ABSOLUTE ACRIMONY

An Alice Campana Mystery

Sue Brletic

This book is dedicated to my late husband, John. I'm sorry it took me so long to follow through in publishing it. You were my biggest cheerleader. I know you are smiling as I complete the process. I still hear your voice, "You need to publish that book!" So here it is! I miss you and hope I make you proud.

Thanks to my family and friends for taking time to read all my rough drafts and also encouraging me to follow through. I love you all!

To Melissa, John & Chelsea: You are my greatest inspiration! I am proud to be your mom.
To Linda: Thanks for pushing me to pursue my dream. That's what sisters do, right?
To Laura: Thank you for giving me the confidence to self publish. It seemed like a daunting task but you helped me to take the plunge!
To Hannah (Left Wright): My book cover is exactly how I envisioned it. You are truly gifted and I can't thank you enough for taking time out of your schedule to create it. Stay tuned for book #2!
To Brad & Lynne: This last year has been a journey, but this family keeps me whole. I love you bro' and my sweet sister-in-law. Thank you also for your support.

"Unless you are good at guessing, it is not much use being a detective." Agatha Christie

"Every man at the bottom of his heart believes that he is a born detective." John Buchan

CONTENTS

ABSOLUTE ACRIMONY

An Alice Campana Mystery

CHAPTER ONE

The residents of Elmwood Manor watched in stunned silence as the paramedics wheeled the body of Carson James to the waiting ambulance. They had witnessed fellow residents of Elmwood being taken out on a gurney in the past, sometimes never to return, but their Director???

Small groups of senior citizens began speculating among themselves as to the cause of Mr. James' death. A heart attack, maybe a stroke, what could possibly have brought about such an early demise?

"I hear he had an allergy to peanuts." Gertrude Smith said. "I'd swear I tasted peanut oil in our stir fry for dinner. Do you suppose someone in the kitchen used peanut oil? They know how many of us are sensitive." She complained to bystanders, addressing no one in particular.

"He was such a young man. I hope he didn't suffer." said Faye Ouellette.

"We should go light a candle for him." Thelma Frank said, heading for the chapel.

Shaking their heads and heading back to the activities they were involved in prior to the excitement, the small groups began to disperse, reflecting on different possibilities.

Alice Campana continued to watch out the front door as the body of Carson James was being driven away to the local hospital. Alice had seen her fair share of bodies, having worked at Elmwood Memorial as a ward secretary. Something wasn't adding up. When the residents were alerted that something was going on in the front office, Alice had been heading towards the library to try to get on the community computer. She watched as a shocked Human Resources manager came out of Mr. James' office, her face ashen and holding her hands over her mouth as she rushed into the nearby ladies' room. Alice knew Jackie to be a grounded employee who kept a calm head during moments of crisis within the facility. Sure, anyone coming upon a dead body would be shocked, but something in Jackie's reaction led Alice to believe there was more to Carson James' death than a mere heart attack.

"No," Alice murmured, "there's more than meets the eye here," as she made her way over to the receptionist's window.

"Oh, hello Alice." Robin Murphy, Elmwood's Administrative Assistant said as she dabbed at her eyes with a wadded-up tissue. "Isn't it horrible?" "I can't believe Carson is dead!"

"Do you know what happened?" Alice asked as she handed Robin a clean tissue from a box on the counter.

"We're not exactly sure. They'll probably do an autopsy for the final cause of death. This is just unbelievable. I was talking to him not even an hour ago and he seemed fine to me. This is just unbelievable." She said again.

"Who found him?"

"Jackie. Ann is with her right now. I guess she is still pretty shaken up."

Ann Lawson was Elmwood's head nurse in the skilled nursing section of the facility.

"Has anyone called Mr. James' next of kin?"

"Oh," Robin said with a start "I never even considered that! I mean, he was always such a private person. I don't think he has any family. I know there isn't a single photo of anyone in his office. Come to think of it, that's a little strange, isn't it? Not even a picture of a cat or dog."

"Well," said Alice, "It's probably all in his personnel file. Jackie will take care of it, I'm sure, once she is up to it."

Alice absently patted Robin's hand and headed toward the infirmary to see if she could find out anything more.

CHAPTER TWO

Alice Campana had been a resident of Elmwood Manor now for the past 5 years. All of 5 feet tall, Alice was a fireball. What she lacked in height she made up in a vibrant personality. Alice maintained a number of wigs, and no one was sure what her real hair looked like. She was a simple, down to earth woman who loved being in the mix of things. She had been one of the original residents who bought an apartment while it was still in Phase One of construction. She sold her family home and rented an apartment on a month-to-month basis while her own apartment was being completed.

The facility now housed over 80 residents in their independent area, plus 48 in assisted living and 30 in their skilled nursing facility. The Manor offered its residents all the comforts of home: including breakfast and dinner every day, laundry services, 24-hour security, exercise rooms and organized activities.

Alice was comfortable with her home and had earned the unofficial title among the residents as "most likely to know" about what was currently going on in the Manor.

Always one to speak her mind, Alice made it her goal to be an ambassador for all the residents and make sure they were getting the most out of their investment. Never married, her only relative in town was her sister Jane's daughter Lucy Amos, a detective in Elmwood's police department.

Lucy was 32, also single, and doggedly determined to work her way up the ranks of the department. She was a beauty, with cropped brown hair, long legs, and cornflower blue eyes. She would stop in and visit with Alice when she was working a case in the area and would often have dinner, spending time with Alice and her friends, entertaining them with stories about some of her past cases. It had been a while since Lucy had been by, so when Alice turned the corner towards the infirmary and nearly ran into Lucy she stopped in her tracks.

"Lucy? What brings you here?" her aunt asked, taking hold of Lucy's arm to steady herself from toppling over.

"Hi, Aunt Alice. Unfortunately, I'm here on business."

"I knew it!" Alice almost shouted. "It's about Carson James, isn't it? How did you get in? I just came from the reception area and didn't see you come in."

"I came through the service entrance. I just got here. I'm trying to find Jackie, have you seen her?"

"Last I heard she was in the infirmary which is down the hall and to your right. I was headed that way myself to see if I could do anything to help. So, there's some funny business going on, right? "

"Aunt Alice," Lucy warned, "you know better than to expect me to answer anything right now. Why don't you head back to your apartment, and I'll check in with you when I'm done here?"

Alice continued holding on to Lucy's arm as she continued down the hallway. "Who called you? Why are you here? Did Jackie kill him? How did she do it?"

Lucy pulled away from her aunt. "Slow down. What makes you think Mr. James was murdered? Aunt Alice, what are you talking about?"

"Never mind," Alice said with a knowing grin. "I'm sure you'll figure it out. I knew she looked suspicious when she was coming out of his office. "

"I want you to go back to your apartment." Lucy said firmly. "No one has said anything to me about a murder. I heard over the scanner that Mr. James had been transported to the hospital DOA so I came by to see if there was anything I could do. Please Aunt Alice don't start making anything more out of this!" Lucy planted a kiss on the top of Alice's head and gently steered her back in the direction of her apartment. "I will come see you in a little while, ok?"

Alice grudgingly headed down the hallway back towards the reception area. Lucy turned on her heel and made her way back towards the infirmary. As she disappeared around the corner, Alice swiveled around and followed Lucy, staying close to the wall.

CHAPTER THREE

As Alice neared the infirmary, she could hear Lucy and Ann quietly talking to Jackie as she haltingly responded through alternate hiccups and sobs. Not wanting to be seen, she looked around for a place to hide and decided to duck into the utility closet whose wall adjoined that of the infirmary's. Closing the door softly behind her, she put her ear against the wall and closed her eyes as if that would help amplify the sound coming from next door.

"…..awful…have never seen someone dead before…..could this have happened?" More hiccups and sobs.

Lucy and Anne murmured softly in response to Jackie's near hysteria.

"I DON'T KNOW!" Jackie unexpectedly shouted. Startled, Alice backed away from the wall and banged her head against some unseen object. "Fudge!" she muttered and ran a hand over her head to see if she could feel any bleeding. Nope. No blood, but she did notice a lump beginning to form.

Silence from the other room. Alice heard movement in the hallway then Lucy's voice ".must have come from outside" and then hearing her voice again coming from the infirmary.

Realizing that her subterfuge was getting her nowhere since she couldn't make enough out of the conversations in the room next door, Alice reached for the handle of the closet only to find the knob would not turn. "Oh, horse feathers!" she moaned. "Now what?" Feeling blindly around trying to find a light switch Alice banged once again into the unseen object.

Within moments, light from the hallway flooded into the closet. "Aunt Alice!" Lucy exclaimed. "What the hell are you doing?" "Language dear," Alice responded as she pulled herself together and managed to extract herself from the closet with as much dignity as she could muster. As Jackie and Ann peered into the hallway, Alice gave them both a weak smile and made her way back to her apartment.

Nearing the reception area, Alice came upon Thelma, Faye and Gertrude staring out the front door. Dusk had fallen and Alice could see red and blue lights strobing through the imminent darkness.

"Oh, Alice!" Faye cried, clutching at her chest. "The police are here now. They're saying that Mr. James' death is "suspicious!" "

"They're probably going to charge the kitchen staff for poisoning him!" Gertrude said dryly. "It was inevitable that someone was going to die from the crap that they serve us!"

"Gertrude don't make jokes at a time like this!" sputtered Thelma. "We should be saying a prayer for Mr. James, God rest his soul."

Alice and her friends watched as a team of men in jumpsuits and booties over their shoes entered Carson James' office, closing the door firmly behind them.

"Show is over, ladies!" a voice from behind them proclaimed. Lieutenant Hector Sharpe, Lucy's boss and Elmwood's answer to Telly Savalas, lollipop and all, gently began to usher them away from the office area.

"Hello Lieutenant. I'm Alice Campana, Lucy's Aunt."

"Mrs. Campana!" he smiled. "...so nice to see you again." Gertrude snorted at the "Mrs." and waited for Alice to fire back that it was "*MS* Campana not *Mrs*." but Alice merely nodded in return. "Will you be wanting our statement?" she queried.

Puzzled, Lieutenant Sharpe asked "And what statement would that be? Is there something you are aware of about Mr. James' death?"

"Hey Lieutenant!" Lucy called from behind the group. "What's going on?"

"Detective Amos, I wasn't aware that they had called you in." Sharpe noted.

"No one called me in. I was in the area and heard about Mr. James' death so thought I'd see if there was anything I could do. What are YOU doing here?"

Motioning towards the library with his lollipop, Lieutenant Sharpe suggested "How about you and I step into the library?"

Lucy followed Lieutenant Sharpe's lead with Alice directly behind her. Lucy stopped, and suppressing a sigh said, "Aunt Alice, I think the Lieutenant meant that he wanted to talk to me privately."

"Look Lucy. I told you there was something funny going on around here. I think Lieutenant Sharpe would be VERY interested in hearing what I have to say."

"Please Auntie, let me handle this for now, please??" Lucy begged. "I know you mean

well, but I really need to get a handle on what is going on."

"Sure," Alice smiled at her niece. "I'll just wait here until he's ready for me."

Rolling her eyes, Lucy headed into the library to meet with her boss.

CHAPTER FOUR

By now the reception area was quickly filling with Elmwood's elderly residents. Pandemonium was beginning to set in. Seniors jockeyed for positions to get a better view of the activity coming from new squad cars arriving at the scene. Ilse Schreiber put her electric wheelchair in reverse, pinning Gabe Stanton against the wall. Howling in pain, Gabe lifted his cane as a defense and sent a vase of flowers crashing to the floor. Ilse shot forward in her chair, sending a patrolman entering the building flat on his back.

"Hot dog!" yelled Gertrude. "I haven't seen this much excitement since the Rangers and Bruins went over the glass and into the stands back in the 70's. What a night that was!"

Suddenly, Lucy and Lieutenant Sharpe came charging out of the library, hands waving in the air trying to restore a semblance of calm. "People, people!" the Lieutenant shouted. "Please return to your rooms. There is nothing to see here. Please let my staff do their job! Go back to your rooms, PLEASE!"

"Anderson, Foster, please make sure these folks get back safely to their rooms. Amos, come with me please."

Lucy searching for her aunt shot her another warning glance and mouthed "Go to your room!" and followed Lieutenant Sharpe into Carson James' office.

Running a hand through his thinning hair, Lieutenant Sharpe groaned "How did we lose control of this situation?" He fumbled in his pocket and withdrew another Tootsie roll pop.

"So, what's it look like in here?" he asked the team who were busy dusting for fingerprints and checking for evidence.

"Would have been better if the body hadn't been moved."

growled one the men from behind a camera he was using to document the scene.

"Seriously, Lieutenant, what are we looking for here? Fill us in. We've got nothing to go by."

"Ok, gang. Here's what I know so far."

As Lucy and the team of investigators continued to go through Carson James' office, Alice, back in her apartment, began pulling out sheets of her embossed stationary so she could start to put together a timeline for Lieutenant Sharpe to begin analyzing. "I knew this ugly stuff would come in handy one day." she said, referring to the lilac colored, lilac scented paper with the scripted "A" centered on the top. The paper was a gift from her "Secret Santa" during last year's gift exchange.

Closing her eyes and picturing what had unfolded before her, she tried to connect the dots of what had been nagging at her from the moment she saw Jackie leave Carson James' office.

There really wasn't a lot of information there, she admitted to herself as she finished writing with only a half of a page of notes. She read and reread what she had written. Yes, it was all there but something in the back of her mind was hanging there, waiting to be pulled from the recesses of her memory. What had she forgotten? Maybe Lucy was right, and she was trying to make something more out of Mr. James' death than there was. But then what were the police doing here? Law enforcement does not show up en masse when someone dies of a heart attack. There had to be a murder! "Murder!" she exclaimed. "Here in Elmwood Manor!" Well, she thought, she would just have to see what Lucy had to say. She brewed herself a cup of hot tea, sat down on her recliner and waited for Lucy to come.

Slowly Alice's eyes began to close. Fighting to stay awake but finally losing the battle she fell into a troubled sleep. The clock above her kitchen sink read 10:05.

CHAPTER FIVE

The dining room was abuzz with dozens of conversations about the prior evening's events.

Faye, Thelma, and Gertrude sat at their usual table, minus Alice.

"Do you think we should call up to her room to see if she's ok?" asked Thelma. "She's never late for breakfast."

Faye nodded in agreement.

"Knowing Alice," Gertrude said, "she's probably heading up the task force as we speak! You know she's not going stay out of the investigat........ Well, look who's here." She said looking up as Alice approached their table.

"Good morning girls. Good morning, Judge" Alice said acknowledging a dour looking resident sitting by herself at the table adjoining theirs. The woman nodded back, picked up her newspaper and headed back to the independent residential area.

"Well looks like she's had her usual dose of prunes this morning." Gertie said. "Why is that woman so darned unfriendly?"

"I hear she's had a lot of tragedy in her life" Faye shared.

"Oh please." Gertie said. "We've all had our crosses, to bear but that doesn't make us as prickly as a porcupine."

"Don't judge people unless you've walked in their shoes...." Faye offered.

Gabe Stanton hobbled over to their table.

"Gabe!" Thelma cried as she stood up. "How are you? Come have a seat with us and get some breakfast."

"I already ate." He grumbled. He shoved a piece of paper at the women.

"What's this?" asked Gertrude, reaching out for the document.

"A petition!" Gabe responded. "I'm trying to get enough signatures to have Ilse Schreiber's electric wheelchair taken from her. That damn woman is going to kill someone yet!"

"Remember when she backed her wheelchair into the Thanksgiving buffet last year? Oooh that beautiful ice sculpture they had as the centerpiece came crashing down. Food and ice chips went everywhere!" Thelma reminisced.

Gertie started laughing. "The look on Chef Lewis's face was priceless. I thought he was actually going to cry. He was able to salvage enough of the food to complete our dinner though. What a champion! How about the time Ilse knocked over the ladder when Ken Scranton was hanging the Christmas garland? I wasn't there but I hear Ken was hanging on to the beam, yelling for someone to replace the ladder."

Gertrude sobered at the thought. "Give me the petition Gabe. I'll definitely sign it!"

As the other ladies began to sign Gabe's petition, Thelma looked at Alice.

"Are you ok dear?" she asked. "You're awfully quiet this morning."

"What?" asked Alice snapping out of her reverie. "Oh, I'm fine. I'm just trying to remember something that I can't put my finger on. So, what's on the menu this morning? Runny eggs or rubber pancakes?"

After breakfast, the foursome headed to the activities room to work on a three-dimensional jigsaw puzzle of Big Ben that they had been building. Although the table was set up so anyone who wanted could participate, the complexity of the puzzle hadn't drawn anyone other than them.

"Whose decision was it to build this monstrosity?" Gertie grumbled. "We've got to be crazy spending so much time on this thing. Every time we put in a piece; 4 pieces fall out. I go to sleep at night with visions of Big Ben on my brain!"

Faye giggled. "'Excellent project for working on your hand/

eye coordination ladies!'" she mimicked their Occupational Therapy coordinator. "I wonder what final arrangements are being made for Mr. James? It seems like the staff is being awfully closed lipped this morning. What did Lucy tell you Alice?"

"Humph!" Alice said. "I waited up practically half the night for her to come see me and she never showed!"

"Poor thing," sympathized Thelma. "You're probably exhausted."

"Oh, I don't seem to need as much sleep as I did when I was younger. Let's take a walk to the reception desk and see if there's any news."

The foursome made their way down to the front of the building, occasionally stopping to confer with other residents who had already been down there to check any updates.

"They think he was strangled!" one resident exclaimed.

"No, it was poison. Definitely poison!" her companion offered.

"No, it was the 'one armed man' (referring to the TV series from the 60's)," Gertrude muttered under her breath. "Well, you ladies have a pleasant day. Probably best to stay in our rooms until they've found the culprit!" she said as the women looked at each other in alarm and scurried to their rooms.

"You are an evil woman, Gertrude Smith!" said Thelma reprovingly.

"At our age, you get your kicks any way you can grab them!" She grinned and headed towards the lobby.

CHAPTER SIX

Gertrude Smith, aka "Gertie" was one of Alice's closest friends. She had moved into the Manor shortly after Alice had settled in and the two of them immediately gravitated towards one another. Even in her late 70s, Gertie was still a stunning looking lady. Her once blonde hair was now died a pale ash color, which she bundled into a top knot. Osteoporosis was taking its toll on her once elegant erect figure, but she still dressed stylishly- sometimes on the eccentric side and carried herself with dignity.

A widow of 10 years, Gertie was finally convinced by her son to sell the palatial estate that she had occupied with her musician/composer husband. Married for 50 years, the couple had traveled the world while Mort, her husband, performed with well-known bands such as Artie Shaw, Glenn Miller, and Harry James to name a few. The two had met at a dance hall where Mort was performing, and Gertie was a co-ed majoring in art at Brown University. Gertie had flushed with pleasure when she noticed the young man on the stage smiling at her when he wasn't engaged in blowing the sweetest trumpet she had ever heard. She nearly fainted when he came towards her between sets to offer to buy her a drink.

The rest, as they say, was history. Gertie dropped out of college to become Mrs. Morton Smith, travelling the world while dabbling occasionally in oils and watercolors.

Gertie sold several her pieces of art. "Sympathy sales." She called them. Friends as well as Harry James himself found her work to be stunning and purchased her paintings sometimes as quickly as she could produce them. However, once she became pregnant with her son, Harry (yes, she named him after Mr. James himself), Gertie put her art aside and focused on becoming the best mother she could be.

When Mort passed away from pancreatic cancer, Gertie rarely ventured out of her home. Sometimes she would pick up a palette and canvas and attempt to create something, only to put it aside. Dozens of unfinished canvasses sat in her studio, while Gertie roamed their empty home. Concerned, Harry begged Gertie to sell the home and move into something smaller. When Harry's company transferred him to Ohio, he put his foot down and told Gertie that she was coming with him.

Tired of the endless arguments with her son, Gertie conceded and after countless hours of looking at senior complexes, decided to make Elmwood Manor her new home.

Faye moved in approximately a year after Gertrude. She was the peace maker of the foursome. Labeled "Miss Switzerland" by Gertrude, Faye hated conflict in any form. Faye lost her husband in an industrial accident when they were in their forties and never remarried. She had raised their four children on her own. Faye, also a petite lady, had curly blonde hair, and still shapely in her mid-70's. With her "baby blue eyes" she appeared naïve and innocent, which for the most part she was, but when crossed could turn into a force to be reckoned with.

Faye provided for her young family by taking in laundry and mending clothes. While they were never rich, she made sure food was always on the table for them. All four children graduated from college with the help of scholarships and student loans. The children had pledged to each other when they were younger that when they were able, they would provide for their mother. True to their word, the four combined their resources and purchased an apartment for Faye at Elmwood Manor. Faye subsidized whatever bills she had left with her social security and a small pension from her husband's company that she received based on a settlement from his accident.

Walking around the Manor the first few days of moving in,

Faye looked like she was in a daze. She smiled shyly at the other residents but looked painfully uncomfortable until Alice and Gertie took her under their wings, making sure she didn't eat alone and had a partner for games night until Faye became more involved with the community. So, when Thelma moved in, Faye took on the role to make sure that Thelma quickly adapted to her new environment.

Thelma was the serious member of the foursome but had a dry sense of humor. Tall and lanky, with short silver hair, Thelma was a simple, no-frills person. She had at one time, been a member of the Poor Clares, or silent nuns. Thelma shared with her new friends that while she thought she had the "calling," having to "beg" and live entirely from donations given to her order by local people eventually got to her. She recalled ending up in a local tavern- habit and all- ordering up a scotch on the rocks, much to the shock of the local patrons, thus ending her proclaimed life of abstinence and poverty. Thelma retained her strong faith in God and would try to rein her friends in when she felt "spiritual guidance" was necessary.

Once Thelma was welcomed into the group – the sisterhood was born.

CHAPTER SEVEN

Robin Murphy was not at the front desk when the foursome arrived. Adam Sams, the day shift security guard was manning the desk.

"Robin called off sick." He said before the ladies even attempted to ask where she was. "I'm filling in for her today and "NO" I have no idea what is going on." Then he returned to reading his newspaper.

"Adam," Alice said. "You've got to know SOMETHING! Come on, we've been friends for years. Fill us in."

Adam raised an eyebrow. "Alice, every time I give you even a morsel of information about what goes on in this place you turn it into personal crusade. I think they're going to be having a meeting in the community room around 1:00. So, if you four can just be patient, I'm sure they'll have all the information you need to know at that time."

"NEED" to know" Alice repeated. "Not necessarily the same as "ought to know."

Adam groaned. "There you go again, Alice, twisting my words around. You know what? I like my job here, so from this moment on my lips are sealed!" Adam physically turned his chair in another direction, appearing to be mesmerized by a painting in front of him.

"Come on girls," said Alice. "We're obviously not going to get anything from HIM! We'll go directly to the source – I'll call Lucy and get the scoop."

"Do you really think Lucy will tell you anything?" asked Thelma doubtfully.

"Probably not," Alice admitted. "I HATE being in the dark. I suppose we'll just have to wait for the meeting and see what bunch of malarkey they're going to feed us."

By 12:45 the community room was filled to capacity. It seemed like every resident in the independent section had arrived and some from assisted living as well. The foursome made their way into the room avoiding walkers, scooters and some canes lying haphazardly across the floor.

Gabe, on the lookout for Ilse, gradually made his way over to Alice and company.

"So, what times does this dog and pony show begin?" he asked gruffly. "I'm gonna be missing my favorite soap if they don't get this thing started soon."

Gertie was about to respond when a familiar voice came over the microphone.

"Hello, ladies and gentlemen. You may remember me. My name is William Dunahie and as many of you may recall, I was the Director of Elmwood Manor up until about a year ago. I have been asked to come back and temporarily fill in for a little while. I know many of you are very anxious to hear about the unfortunate situation that occurred yesterday. While it's very nice to see so many familiar faces, I'm sorry that we have to meet again under such sad circumstances."

"As most of you already know, Carson James, passed away very unexpectedly early last evening. The Elmwood Police Department believes that foul play may have been involved in his death."

A murmur rose through the crowd, gradually building to louder conversations between groups of residents.

"What is this world coming to?" "I wonder if we're in any danger?" "Who could have done such a thing?" were some of the comments heard over the din.

Mr. Dunahie held his arms up placatingly to the crowd. "Now I know this is very upsetting news, but we wanted to assure you that we firmly believe that this is a single incident. We do not believe that any of you here at the Manor are in any danger. The police are working on some solid leads and feel they should come to a quick resolution."

"So how did he die?" asked Charlie Greene.

"At this point, we really are very limited as to what information we can release at this point." Said Mr. Dunahie. "However, Lieutenant Sharpe is here to answer any questions he can at this time. Lieutenant Sharpe?"

"Good afternoon, everyone. My name is Lieutenant Hector Sharpe with the Elmwood Police Department, and this is Detective Lucy Amos. We'd like to give you the information that we are aware of at this time. As Mr. Dunahie mentioned, it does appear that Mr. James' death was a result of foul play. Right now, we are unable to go into too many specifics due to the sensitivity of the case. We have a team dedicated to evaluating the evidence and feel we should be able to come to a satisfactory conclusion here soon."

"Blah, blah, blah…" interrupted Gabe. "We all watch CSI too. Cut to the chase and give us the skinny. How did he kick?"

Lucy coughed and hid a smile behind her hand.

"At this point we believe Mr. James may have been poisoned. From what we can tell, it appears that he may have ingested something, but we are currently waiting for the toxicology report."

Alice stiffened at this news and glanced at Jackie to gauge her reaction. Jackie looked down at the floor and wiped at her eyes with a tissue. Alice raised her hand and asked, "Do you have any idea who may have done this?"

"Again, we have some possible leads we are pursuing but nothing conclusive at present."

"Will you be asking us for our statements?" Alice asked again. "I think I have something you will find very interesting." Jackie's head snapped up at this point, and looked at Alice, eyebrows raised.

"Of course, we will be more than happy to talk to anyone who feels they may have something to help us. Mr. Dunahie, is there a room we could use for the next few days?"

"I'll make sure that we do, Lieutenant." Mr. Dunahie replied.

"Well then." Sharpe said, "Let us make some arrangements to begin interviewing those of you who feel they have something to contribute. Detective Amos and I will start tomorrow. Please stop by and see us at the end of this meeting so we can put together a list. If there is anything you can remember about last night, no matter how insignificant it may seem we would be very interested in talking to you. I know there is very little information to give you, but please know we are making this case our top priority. Thank you all for coming and for your patience and cooperation."

As the residents began shuffling out of the room, Gertie turned to Alice and said, "What do you know that we don't know?"

"Really!" Faye exclaimed. "Did you see something Alice?"

"Not here." Alice said, glancing around the room. "Let's go back to my apartment and talk. First, let me get on the list for tomorrow and see if I can get Lucy to give me a little more info."

Alice approached Lucy who was talking with Mr. Dunahie and Lieutenant Sharpe. The group stopped talking and waited for her to speak.

"Lucy." Alice said. "Lieutenant. It's nice to see you again Mr. Dunahie. I haven't seen you since you were fired – uh – left us last year."

"Hello Ms. Campana. It's nice to see you again. You're looking well."

"A lot better than Mr. James did when he was wheeled out of here!" Alice retorted.

"Aunt Alice!" Lucy said reprovingly.

"So, Ms. Campana, you have some information you would like to share with us?" asked the Lieutenant.

"I sure do! I'll bet you'll have this case solved in a jiffy once you hear what I have to say. I can take a ride in your squad car and come down to the station and make my statement tonight if you want. Just don't give me any coffee. I hear the coffee there is terrible. Personally, I like a nice hot cup of tea. Do you have tea bags there? If not, I can go to my room and get a couple and bring them with me."

Lieutenant Sharpe smiled at Alice. "As much as I appreciate your enthusiasm, Mrs. – um Ms. Campana, I think tomorrow will work just fine for us to speak. How about if we put you first on our list? If you can come to the front desk around 9:00 tomorrow morning you will have our undivided attention."

"Well 9:00 is usually our shopping trip time but I think I can skip it tomorrow. Will you be there too Lucy?" she asked.

"Yes, I'll be here." Lucy answered.

"Well, I mean I wasn't sure if that would be like a conflict of interest or anything with me being your aunt and all. I guess that's why you didn't come see me last night like you said you would."

"Actually, I did stop by your apartment last night," Lucy said. "I got there about 10:45 and you were sound asleep in your favorite chair. I tried to wake you, but you were sleeping so soundly I didn't push it. I covered you with your afghan and left."

Alice thought for a moment. "I kind of remember now that you mention it. Must have been the turkey we had for dinner last night. Did you know there's something in turkey that makes you sleepy? I mean think about it. Doesn't everyone want to take a nap right after Thanksgiving dinner?"

Alice said good-bye to the group and went to meet up with her friends.

"Interesting woman…." Mr. Dunahie murmured.

CHAPTER EIGHT

The foursome sat at Alice's kitchen table, drinking coffee (hot tea for Alice) and sampling a new cookie recipe Alice had found and ripped out of a magazine at her doctor's office.

"Very good!" Thelma said as she reached for another.

"I'm glad they turned out." Alice said. "I couldn't find the last part of the recipe because someone had taken a coupon on the other side of the page, so I had to improvise. Some people are so inconsiderate!"

"I'm dying to find out what you know about Mr. James' death – pardon the pun." said Gertie. "The suspense is killing me! I'm on pins and needles…"

"Enough already!" said Faye. "Come on Alice – fill us in please!!!"

Alice got up from the table and brought back the notes she had put together. "I'm pretty sure once Lieutenant Sharpe sees this – the case will be solved!" She proceeded to tell the other ladies about Jackie's suspicious behavior. "It's obvious she is responsible for poisoning Mr. James." She said as she finished reviewing her notes. "It all fits. The Lieutenant said Mr. James was poisoned with something. Well, who has access to drugs here at the Manor? Jackie Drake for starters…. she has keys to everything here, including the cabinet where they lock up all the medications! When I saw her come out of his office, she looked as guilty as a cat that swallowed the canary!"

"But WHY would Jackie want to kill Carson James?" asked Thelma. "They always appeared to be comfortable around each other. She was his right-hand man – so to speak!"

"That's what we have to find out!" Alice exclaimed. "Once we find the motive, all the pieces will fit together. Kind of like our Big Ben puzzle....one piece at a time!"

"And how do you propose that we do that?" asked Gertie suspiciously.

"Funny you should ask." Alice smiled. "I've got a plan!"

Thelma shook her head doubtfully. "I don't know Alice. The last time you had "a plan" they had to stop the shuttle bus and have the rescue squad get involved."

"That was just an unfortunate accident." Alice said defending herself. "Who would have thought that the air freshener spray would be so potent? It sure looks like it works on TV Actually, it was still better than having to smell Jack Wellington's farts. That man should have a plug installed up his butt as a community service. And anyway, once everyone was cleared out of the shuttle and the windows were opened, we were on our way within a half an hour!"

"It certainly gave everyone something to talk about for the rest of the week!" Faye laughed. "So, what is your plan?"

Alice spent the next 30 minutes going over the details and delegating what part each of them would play.

CHAPTER NINE

By 8:30 most residents were settled in their rooms for the evening. Day staff were gone, and a skeleton evening staff were usually in place by 9:00.

Three of the team were back in Alice's apartment, waiting for Gertie. After a soft tap on the door, Gertie quickly entered the room, glancing over her shoulder. She was wearing a black turtleneck, black hoodie, black slacks, and black shoes. All three ladies were looking at her.

"What?" she asked. "I dressed for the occasion. This is what all the super sleuths are wearing these days!"

"You look like cat woman!" Thelma said giggling.

"Ok," said Alice. "Does everyone remember what to do?"

"I am so nervous." Faye said. "Are you sure we should do this?"

"Oh Faye, grow a pair!" Alice snapped irritably. "You've had all afternoon to back out and we're down to the wire so suck it up!"

"I'm not going to back out. I just said I was nervous, that's all."

"I'm nervous too, if that helps." said Thelma. "Let's just do it and get it over!"

"Everyone synchronize their watches." Alice said. "I have 8:29."

"I have 8:30," said Faye.

"I have 8:32." said Thelma. "Maybe we should call time and temp and find out who is right!"

"Oh, for heaven sakes!" Alice groaned. "Let's all just make it 8:30 ok??"

Watches set and synchronized the women set off down the hallway. As they neared the front desk, they split off in pairs:

Thelma and Faye heading towards the front desk with Gertrude and Alice staying back around the corner.

"Hello Adam, hello Frank." said Thelma. "Getting ready to go home Adam?"

"Is there something you ladies need?" asked Frank.

"Well, as a matter of fact there is." Said Faye. "Thelma and I were just discussing what kind of degree you two had to have to become security guards. I said you probably had to go to a police academy and Thelma said you had to have a degree in criminal justice. We both agree that we are very lucky to have such big strong men to look out for us!"

Both men noticeably adjusted their posture, pushing their chest out and flexing without trying to appear to do so.

"Look at those guns!" said Thelma admiringly. "Would you mind if we felt them?"

Alice pantomimed putting her finger down her throat to Gertrude, while the other two continued their diversion.

With both guards facing the front counter, Alice and Gertie quietly opened the side door to the office and tip toed inside. Each took a different area of the room until Gertie motioned to Alice that she had found what they were looking for. Shutting the door quietly behind them, they joined their friends at the counter.

"There you two are!" exclaimed Alice. "I thought we were going to meet in the community room and work on our puzzle!"

"You ladies are up late this evening," said Frank.

"Oooh," shuddered Faye. "We all have been SOOO upset about Mr. James that none of us can sleep. We thought if we worked on our puzzle, it may help us to relax a little. It was very nice chatting with you! Thanks once again for keeping us safe. It's nice to know we are in such good hands!"

Waving goodbye to Frank and Adam, Alice and company headed back down the hallway.

"Did you find them?" Thelma whispered.

Gertie held up a set of keys in her hand, smiling triumphantly.

"Put them away!" Alice hissed. "Someone may see us!"

Gertie put the keys in her pocket, glancing over her shoulder to make sure no one was around. "Step one accomplished!" she grinned.

CHAPTER TEN

The team turned the lights on in the community room and pretended to be engrossed in working on their project.

"How did we do?" Thelma asked.

"You poured it on a little thick there," said Alice "but you were definitely effective!"

"Men are such dopes!" Faye said. "'Can I feel your muscles?' " she mimicked Thelma.

"They *were* pretty impressive!" Thelma replied.

"Ok girls – focus!" Alice said. "We're only halfway there to accomplishing our mission. Adam should be leaving soon if he hasn't already. Frank usually makes his rounds about 9:30. After he finishes the first floor, he takes the elevator to the second then third floor. I figure we have about 30 to 45 minutes top to find what we are looking for."

"What ARE we looking for?" Faye asked.

"I don't know." Alice admitted. "But I'll know it when I see it. You and Thelma continue to work on the puzzle. If you see Frank heading towards the office, I want you to let Gertie and I know."

"How are we going to do that?" asked Thelma

"By using these!" she said, proudly producing 2 walkie talkies. Where on earth did you get these?" asked Gertie.

"Lucy bought them for me a few years ago. She took me to Las Vegas and was worried she'd lose me in the casinos. So, we carried these around with us so we could stay in contact."

"I'm impressed!" Gertie said. "Lucy always thinks of everything. I sure wish she and my son would hook up. They would be perfect for each other. Both work so hard and take no time to play."

"Lucy is not interested in men right now." Alice replied. "According to her, her career comes first – men later. But we'll definitely work on at least introducing them." Alice spent the next five minutes showing them how to turn the walkie talkies on and off, adjust the volume and which button to push to talk.

"I remember when I met Mort." Gertie reminisced. "I was sure I was going to spend my life showing my art, opening up my own gallery and boom there he was! Love works in mysterious ways!"

"Earth to Gertie!" Alice said, snapping her fingers in front of Gertie's face. "Can we just focus on what we're doing here? Geez...."

"You ladies ok in here?" Frank asked from the doorway.

Startled, Thelma turned and flung her walkie talkie across the room.

"What's that?" Frank asked.

"Oh, just some toy one of the grandkids left behind during visitation." Faye replied quickly.

"Hmmm. Well ok. I'm heading off towards my rounds so I'll catch up with you later. Don't stay up too late now!" he said as he headed towards the first-floor residential area.

"Sorry," said Thelma, heading over to pick up the walkie talkie. "I didn't even hear him coming. I didn't realize how much I'm on edge!"

"Hmph!" Gertie said. "You two have the easy part. Alice and I are the ones who should be nervous. Speaking of which, are you ready Alice?"

"Give Frank a few more minutes. Once we hear the elevator ding, we'll know he's heading up to the second floor. Faye, why don't you head towards your room. It's the closest to the elevator so if Frank sees you, he won't suspect anything. When you hear him get on the elevator, come back and let us know."

Ten minutes later, Faye was back in the community room giving them the thumbs up.

"Here we go!" said Alice, "commencing phase two! Remember, don't forget to let us know if you hear Frank coming!"

Fingering the walkie talkie nervously, Thelma nodded.

CHAPTER ELEVEN

Alice and Gertie headed back toward the front desk, stopping at Jackie Drake's office door. Gertie handed Alice the keys they had taken, and Alice began trying the different keys into the lock. "Hurry up!" Gertie whispered glancing around. A few minutes later she heard the click as Alice finally found the right key.

"Success!" Alice beamed.

They both stepped into the dark office, shutting the door quietly behind them.

"Do you have the flashlights?" she asked Gertie.

"Um, they're still sitting on your kitchen table."

"You've got to be kidding me! How are we supposed to snoop around in the dark?"

"Let's just turn on her light." Gertie fumbled around and a few seconds later, Jackie's overhead lights flickered on. Taking off her black hoodie and tucking it around the bottom of the door, Gertie said "I saw someone do this on a cop show I was watching the other day. This way, no one can see the light from under the door!"

"Well, you better hope it works!" Alice shot back. "I can't believe you forgot the flashlights. Ok - less talking and more snooping. You take the file cabinets over there and I'll start going through her desk. If you see anything that looks suspicious, put it one of these bags," she said handing Gertie a Stop N Shop plastic bag.

"What else do you have in those pockets?" asked Gertie. "Walkie talkies, plastic bags.... tell me you're not armed!"

"Don't be ridiculous!" Alice sniffed. "But I did bring my pepper spray!"

Shaking her head, Gertie headed towards Jackie's file cabinets.

"All I see in here are just lots of files. They all seemed to be alphabetized......Acme Vending, Airport receipts, BMV – this could take all night!"

"Well, we don't have all night so do the best you can" answered Alice going through Jackie's top drawer. "Nothing here but staplers, tape, white out.... Let's see what's in drawer two. Well, one thing I have discovered is that Jackie has a sweet tooth! Look at all these candy bars and M & M bags! I bet her dentist loves her!"

"Bingo!" said Gertie. "I found the personnel file drawer. I can't believe she doesn't have it locked- and lookee here – Carson James' file!"

"Put it in your bag!" said Alice. "At least we got something! There's nothing in her drawers other than the usual desk stuff. You sure you didn't miss anything else important in those files?"

"Well, I can't be sure," replied Gertie, "but other than the personnel files, it all looked like the usual stuff you'd see in a file cabinet. Hmmm...she said reading over Carson James' file, do know how much they were PAYING him?"

"Gertie! We can read that later. Keep looking! What time do you have?"

"9:45 – how about you?"

"Ditto. We're running out of time! What are we missing? Wish I could hack into her computer, but I have no idea what her password is."

Gertie headed over to Jackie's desk and stood by Alice looking at the computer screen. "I'm lucky if I know how to turn one of these things on, let alone figure out her password! Scoot over." Gertie gently pushed Alice aside and removed the top drawer.

"What are you doing?" asked Alice.

"Just wait." Gertie replied. Getting on her knees she began feeling behind where the drawer had been. Doing the same with the second drawer, she was about to replace it when she felt underneath the drawer itself and came up with an envelope that had been taped to it!

"What have we here?" she asked waving the envelope at Alice.

"Let me see that!" Alice said, grabbing the envelope out of Gertie's hand. Colored photographs spilled out of the envelope. Staring down at the pictures, Alice and Gertie saw Carson James and Jackie Drake looking right back at them!

Scooping the pictures up and shoving them in her bag, Alice pointed at her watch and said, "I think we better get out of here. Frank's got to be done by now."

Gertie whirled around and put her hand over Alice's mouth. "Shhh." she whispered.

Frank could be heard whistling off key and apparently heading towards the office door.

Alice hurried over to the door, turned the knob to lock it and flicked off the wall switch. Breathing heavily, the two leaned against the wall while they heard Frank trying to turn the doorknob. Moments later, comfortable that the office was locked, Frank could be heard heading back to the front desk. Giving it a few more minutes, Alice opened the door, motioned for Gertie to follow and high tailed it back to the Community Room.

"I thought I told you to let us know when you saw Frank coming back!" she admonished Faye and Thelma.

"We have been trying to reach you," Thelma said, "but you weren't answering! We have been worried to death!"

Alice reached into her pocket to retrieve her walkie talkie. Sheepishly she showed it to the other women. The power light was not lit. She had forgotten to turn it back on when she was showing them how to work theirs.

Faye sank into a chair. "I don't know about you guys, but I could use a stiff drink!"

"Make that a double!" agreed Thelma. "Tell me you were able to find something so this wasn't all for nothing!"

Alice pulled the pictures out of her Stop N Shop bag, turned them around so Thelma and Faye could see them, and then just as quickly shoved them back in the bag.

Thelma crossed herself. "Geez Louise! Is that who I think it is?"

"Yup!" said Alice grinning. "Let's go back to my place so we can take a good, close look."

CHAPTER TWELVE

The pictures of Carson James and Jackie Drake lay scattered on Alice's kitchen table.

"When do you think these were taken?" asked a puzzled Faye.

"Remember when Mr. James took a vacation around February and Jackie requested a family medical leave around the same time because her mother was 'sick'?" recalled Alice. "I remember when she returned about a week or so after Mr. James came back from vacation how tan she looked. I even asked her where her mother lived. She told me Minnesota and when I mentioned her tan, she said she had been going to a tanning booth while there for some quiet time and to get some color before she started to wear her spring clothes. We all knew Mr. James had been to the Caribbean so it was obvious why he would come back tan. Looks like Mr. James had a travelling companion!"

"Sure looks like it." agreed Gertie. "Palm trees, sandy beaches, ocean views…. looks like quite a place. Reminds me of times I spent in Acapulco when I was travelling with Mortie and the band. I can still feel the ocean breeze on my skin," she said wistfully.

"Well Jackie sure is showing a lot of skin herself!" exclaimed Thelma dryly. "Who'd have thought she was hiding a body like that under her work clothes? Don't they look like the happy couple?" she said looking at a picture with Jackie in a bikini top and sarong with Carson grinning at her holding a drink with an umbrella and wearing a tropical shirt, shorts and sandals.

"And will you look at those coconuts!" Gertie remarked.

"Gertie!" Faye laughed.

"What? I'm talking about THOSE coconuts, she said innocently, pointing to a palm directly behind the couple."

Other photos showed the couple posing in front of fountains, street side cafes, and dancing on a torch-lit beach surrounded by other couples, bonfires, and tables laden with food.

Alice gathered the pictures and put them back into the envelope. "Well, we know that Mr. James and Jackie were definitely involved this winter.   Do you think they are – were – still seeing each other when he was murdered?"

Faye shook her head. "I don't think so. Unless she is a good actress, Jackie hasn't been herself for the last month or so. Haven't you noticed how much weight she has lost? She hasn't seemed happy for quite a while."

Thelma nodded in agreement. "Now that you mention it, I would agree. She has seemed different."

"Regardless," said Faye, "what does it prove anyway?"

"'Hell hath no fury like a woman scorned.'" quoted Thelma.

"It certainly could be a motive."

"For murder?" asked a shocked Faye. "I'm sorry, but I just can't see Jackie as a murderer."

"The next thing we have to figure out is HOW he was murdered," said Alice matter-of-factly. "Then we'll know what murder weapon to look for."

Gertie snorted. "Oh, ok, Alice. I'm sure Jackie has it conveniently hidden for us to find it. What do you think the Police are doing at this moment? If there is anything to be found – they'll be the ones to come up with it."

"Oh, I don't know," sighed Faye, plopping down in Alice's sofa. "I think this is just a little much for the 4 of us to tackle. Let's just let the police do their job. We better turn over the pictures to them, so we're not arrested for withholding evidence."

"Not quite yet," said Alice stuffing the envelope of pictures back in the Stop N Shop bag. "We've only just got started!" She then pulled Carson James' personnel file out of the bag.

"What is THAT?" said Faye trying to pull herself out of the sofa. "Hey, a little help here!"

Thelma held out her hand and pulled Faye to her feet. "Geez

Alice, how do you get yourself off that thing? It's like quicksand!"

"Oh, I don't sit on the sofa. I leave that for company." She said absently while sorting through the folder. "Gertie found Mr. James' personnel folder in Jackie's file cabinet. Let's see if we can find any goodies in here."

Alice passed around pages from the file to each of her cohorts. "Maybe we should take some notes on what we think may be relevant to the case." She said handing each of the ladies a sheet of her lilac scented stationary.

"What the heck is this?" sniffed Gertie. "Good heavens Alice, you don't actually send this to anyone do you?"

"What's wrong with it?" asked Thelma indignantly. "I think it's beautiful."

"Ah ha!" crowed Alice. "So, YOU were my Secret Santa!"

Blushing, Thelma looked down at her piece of stationary and muttered "Some people have no taste!"

"All right ladies!" Faye said. "Let's get back to business. I don't know about the rest of you, but my eyes are almost at half-mast. I'd like to go through this stuff before I turn into a pumpkin!"

Everyone nodded in agreement and bent to their task of examining the sheets they held.

"Well, he graduated from the University of Michigan with a Bachelor of Science and then went on and got his master's degree from the University of Illinois."

"Looks like he was a member of Pi Kappa Alpha fraternity. My son was a "Pike" said Gertie. They even had a fire truck they rode around on campus! 'I'm glad I'm a good Pi K A, I'm glad I'm a good Pi K A, I love all my brothers, to hell with the others, I'm glad I'm a good Pi K A!'" she recited heartily.

The other 3 women looked at Gertie as if she had lost her mind.

"Hmmmm.... on his life insurance application it just names "estate" as his beneficiary. Didn't he have any family?" asked Faye looking back at a sheet she held.

"You know Robin mentioned that there were no pictures in

his office and was wondering the same thing."

"Well, I wonder who will collect on his insurance?" Thelma pondered. "I'm looking at his paysheets – the guy made some good money! Wouldn't it be nice if he left some of to the Church?"

"Yeah right," Gertie said sarcastically, "Mr. James did not strike me as a philanthropist or doer of good deeds."

"I don't know," sighed Alice rubbing the bridge of her nose and laying her eyeglasses aside. "Maybe Jackie would know more about any family or what his final wishes would be. Lucy and Lieutenant Sharpe will be interviewing her. If they aren't aware of their relationship, we may just have to drop a few hints their way."

"Well," said Faye as she stretched her arms in front of her, "this old broad is going to bed. I don't think we're going to solve this thing in one night. Alice, are you going to be in charge of keeping all this stuff together?"

"Sure. I'll lock it up in my safe. We can look at again tomorrow when we're all fresh."

The foursome said their good-nights and Alice locked her door behind them, sliding the top latch into place. After putting coffee mugs and glasses into her dishwasher, washing her face, and brushing her teeth, she climbed into her bed. She lay there staring at the ceiling, trying to sort through all the pieces of the Carson James puzzle. Something continued to pull at the back of her mind. Turning on her side, she closed her eyes and prayed she would have pleasant dreams as a dark figure made its way down the dimly lit hallway knowing they definitely would be having pleasant dreams this evening!

CHAPTER THIRTEEN

The next morning William Dunahie looked around at what used to be his office almost a year ago to the day. The room was in total chaos, with fingerprint residue on furniture, light switches, and every imaginable surface. Pictures were hanging at an angle; the couch cushions were thrown to the side and his once orderly domain looked as if someone had come in with a wrecking ball. "Well Mr. Carson James, looks like your reign was short-lived." He chuckled at his play on words.

When he received the phone call from Corporate Headquarters informing him that he was needed back at Elmwood Manor, it was all he could do to contain himself. He made the appropriate sounds of shock and distress over James' passing and 'grudgingly' agreed to come back and take up his old position. The past year had been pure hell, working with his superiors performing administrative tasks that any clerical staff could have handled. Hell – even a monkey could be trained to do the menial jobs he had been doing, all because somebody had blown the whistle on him and after an investigation, he had his Directorship taken away. But he had swallowed his pride and knew that his day would come once again – and it did! Although he had been warned that his return to the Manor was just temporary, Bill Dunahie knew if he played his cards right, Elmwood Manor would be his once again! He vowed to be the epitome of professionalism and would "schmooze" his way into the hearts of Elmwood Manor's residents, starting with that pesky Alice Campana!

Having received the green light from the sexy Detective Amos and Lieutenant Sharpe, he began putting his office together again. "Just like Humpty Dumpty." He grinned.

CHAPTER FOURTEEN

Boarding the shuttle bus with her eco-friendly shopping bags, Alice looked up to see Faye waving her over to an empty seat beside her. "Missed you at breakfast."

"I'm moving a little slower than usual." Alice said, rubbing her neck. "I must have slept wrong. Looks like everyone needs groceries today," she said looking around the almost full shuttle. "Where are the others?"

"Gertie and Thelma gave me a list of a few items to pick up for them. It's silly for all of us to take up half our day. I would have gotten what you needed too, but I didn't get a chance to ask you."

"It's ok. It feels good to get out of there for a while."

"Yeah, things are a little tense right now. Looks like Mr. Dunahie has picked up where he left off."

"That man gives me the willies!" Alice shivered.

"I hear he went into rehab for a few months and that he's been sober for almost 9 months now."

"Hmph…we'll see," said Alice skeptically. "I can't imagine that they are going to let him run the Manor again. Things are really going down the crapper around here."

Faye laughed. "Our own little Peyton Place! I saw Jackie this morning. She looks awful."

"Yeah, guilt will do that to you."

"You're serious. You really think she killed him, don't you?"

"She had the motive, and she had the opportunity. It looks pretty obvious to me."

"Time will tell."

The residents of Elmwood Manor began disembarking from the shuttle bus to do their weekly grocery shopping. Alice got up from her seat, turned and found herself face to face with Judge Audrey Lambert and hastily sat down again, dropping her bags in the process. The Judge scowled at her and proceeded out of the bus. "Well excuse me!" Alice mumbled as she picked her bags up off the floor.

Alice and Faye made their way down each aisle of their local Kroger's. Checking their lists, they managed to fill up their carts rather quickly.

"I got everything I need," said Faye. "How about you?"

"Looks like it," said Alice. "Want to grab a cup of coffee and a donut at the café?"

Sipping on their drinks and listening to the Muzak in the background, the ladies watched as the other shoppers continued to find the best prices, matching their coupons to the items on their lists.

"I hear Betty George spent only ten cents last week on her groceries after using all her coupons. Can you imagine?"

"I think Betty George needs to get a life!" snapped Alice.

"Amen!" said Judge Audrey Lambert pulling up a chair and sitting down.

Alice and Faye sat in stunned silence as the Judge began adding cream and sweetener into her coffee. "It's like buying a boat – if you have to worry about how much it costs to fill it up, you shouldn't be buying the boat! Couponing is a bunch of nonsense in my eyes. The amount of time it takes clipping the coupons, filing them, and deciding which ones you're going to use could be time better spent!"

Faye nodded in agreement still too stunned to speak.

"Shuttle's leaving in 5 minutes." Adding another pack of sweetener, she then snapped a lid on her cup, got up from the table and headed toward the cash register.

"Well, I'll be damned!" Faye said and then clapped her hands over her mouth. "Sorry," she said.

Alice laughed. "First time I've ever heard you swear Faye, but if you wouldn't have said it- I would have!"

As they headed towards the waiting shuttle bus, they could

hear the sound of breaking glass. Moments later the Muzak was interrupted by "Clean Up in Aisle 6!" Ilse Schreiber rounded the corner in her scooter leaving a trail of spaghetti sauce behind her.

"Did you sign Gabe's petition?" asked Alice.

"Not yet, but it looks like he's going to get a few more signatures," Faye said motioning with her head towards two of the Manor's residents walking slowly towards the exit, their legs and shoes covered with Ragu.

CHAPTER FIFTEEN

Alice was greeted at the door of Elmwood Manor by her niece. "Aunt Alice! Where have you been? Did you forget you were going to meet with Lieutenant Sharpe at 9? What is that smell?" she sniffed as a number of residents who had gotten off the bus walked past her.

"Ilse decided to give us all a little taste of Italy for the ride back from Kroger's. Sorry dear. I totally forgot about my appointment. So much is going on around here it totally slipped my mind. Is he still waiting for me?"

"No. He waited for an hour, talked to some other residents and staff then headed back to the Station. What exactly did you want to tell him anyway?"

"Oh my!" Lucy laughed as the two victims of Ilse's latest mishap were being escorted back to their rooms by the bus driver. "I hope no one was hurt!"

Alice glanced out the front door of the Manor watching as Ken Stanton began hosing down the tires of Ilse's scooter. Ilse, sitting on a nearby bench, sheepishly waved at Alice and Lucy. "No – no one was hurt but I'm thinking if Ken sprays that water a little higher and short circuits her controls, there's a good chance he could take care of that scooter once and for all!"

Alice linked her arm with Lucy's and headed towards her apartment. "Let's go have a cup of tea and talk about the case!"

Opening her apartment door, Alice headed toward the stove to put her kettle on for tea.

"What's all this stuff?" Lucy asked looking at the file folder and envelope of pictures on Alice's kitchen table.

Alice gasped and hurried to the table and began scooping up

the papers. "Oh, nothing dear. I was just going through some old files and pictures last night and forgot to refile them."

"Interesting!" Lucy said grabbing the Carson James folder out of Alice's hand. "Why would YOU have a folder on Carson James? Aunt Alice, I think you need to sit down and start explaining what is going on here."

Alice groaned and sat down heavily on one of her kitchen chairs, putting her head in her hands. "I KNEW I forgot something last night before I went to bed," she muttered.

"Aunt Alice?"

"Oh, all right! The girls and I decided we were going to help you and Lieutenant Sharpe gather evidence. We broke into Jackie's office last night and this is the stuff we found."

Now Lucy put her own head in her hands. "Oh lovely! Now my dear, sweet Aunt is adding burglary to her list of hobbies. Aunt Alice do you realize the trouble you are in?"

"Only if someone finds out," Alice ventured. "Really Lucy all we did was go through some of her drawers. We were going to put it all back!"

"And how were you planning on doing that? By the way, how did you get into her office in the first place? Wasn't it locked?"

"Well, these definitely helped," she said dangling the keys they took from the office between her fingers. "I hadn't figured out how we were going to return them. That was on my list of things to do today."

"Was it now?" Lucy asked sarcastically.

"But Lucy," Alice said excitedly. "Do you know Carson James and Jackie had a "thing" going on? Look at the pictures! No one here at the Manor had any clue. I'll bet he dumped her, and she killed him to get revenge. And did you know Carson James doesn't appear to have any family? Who is going to handle his affairs? By the way, the man made darn good money!"

Despite herself, Lucy began leafing through the photos in the envelope. Pausing every now and then to examine a certain picture, she questioned, "I wonder where and when these were taken?"

"We think it was in February when Mr. James went on vacation. Jackie took a leave of absence around the same time to stay with her "sick mother.""

"That was only a little over 3 months ago. Do you know if they were still involved?"

"We don't think so. Jackie hasn't been herself lately, so we figure he gave her the boot!"

"Or SHE gave HIM the boot," reminded Lucy. "It could work either way."

Snapping back into Detective mode, Lucy shook her head. "I've got to figure out what to do with this stuff. You really put me into a predicament."

"Well," rationalized Alice. "Have you had an opportunity to search Jackie's office yet? Maybe you can say that YOU found the pictures and that you wanted to look at Carson James' personnel file. That could work!" she finished smugly.

"First of all, why would I even WANT to search Jackie's office? And where, by the way, did you find the pictures?"

"Taped underneath one of her drawers," Alice admitted.

Massaging her temples, Lucy sat back in the chair and sighed. "And where did you get the keys pray tell?"

"We are the masters of distraction!" Alice said proudly. "While Thelma and Faye kept Adam and Frank busy, Gertie and I took them from the office."

"This keeps getting worse!" groaned Lucy.

The two sat in silence pondering what to do next. "Give me this stuff. I need to think this over a bit. Aunt Alice you must swear to me that you will NOT do this again! I can see my next promotion going down the drain...."

"Oh, honey!" Alice exclaimed. "I will confess what I did to Lieutenant Sharpe. I don't want to be responsible for you having to walk a beat again."

Lucy laughed. "I never 'walked a beat' Aunt Alice and I don't intend to anytime soon. Look, I am going to take care of this against my better judgment. Just promise me that you and your friends will stay out of this from here on out!"

Alice looked down at her lap and nodded solemnly. "Scout's honor!"

CHAPTER SIXTEEN

After Lucy left her apartment, Alice realized that she had gotten absolutely no information from her. She also realized that she had to come clean with the others that they were "busted." "Some stool pigeon I am!"

She then took out her 'timeline' once again and added the few facts that they had come to learn over the last 12 hours. "Well, it least it wasn't a total loss," she muttered. "We now know that Jackie and Mr. James were a couple at one time and that he has no family. So, what does that mean?" she pondered. "Not a whole lot!"

Dropping the paper on the table, she made her way back into the kitchen to put away her groceries and then planned to go meet up with her friends. Dinner time would be in less than an hour.

Alice met up with Faye 45 minutes later as she also was preparing to enter the dining room.

"We've certainly had a full day so far, haven't we?" asked Faye, looping her arm through Alice's.

"You have no idea!"

"Why, what else has happened?" Faye asked as they made their way to their usual table.

"Let's wait until the others get here and then I'll tell you all."

"Now you've aroused my curiosity!"

"Remember, 'curiosity killed the cat'," quoted Thelma walking up beside them. "What are you curious about Faye?"

"Alice has something to tell us," said Faye as she sat down at the table and proceeded to examine the night's menu. She started laughing. "How appropriate! Spaghetti and meatballs!"

"What's so funny about spaghetti and meatballs?" asked Gertie joining the ladies.

Faye told the others about Ilse's Kroger incident as the server made her way around the table taking their drink orders.

Gertie roared with laughter. "I always seem to miss out on the exciting outings! "

"Well, I don't know how exciting it was," Alice said. "I wonder if Carol and Joan will be able to get the spaghetti sauce out of their clothing!"

Kelly Martin, the young high school student assigned to wait on their table, came back with a tray of salads and their iced teas. Wearing her auburn hair tied back in a ponytail she looked like the young Irish actress portrayed in the Irish Spring soap commercial. She was a natural beauty.

"Well, Miss Kelly," Gertie smiled. "How are you doing this evening?"

"Great Mrs. Smith. Thanks for asking. Prom is this weekend, so you'll probably have someone else taking care of you. I know it's your Memorial Day party as well so I'm sure you won't even miss me," she smiled.

"How exciting!" gushed Faye. "tell us about your dress and how you're going to do your hair. Are you getting your nails done? What shoes are you wearing? Who is your date?"

"Geez Faye," muttered Alice. "What is this, Twenty Questions?"

"Oh, Alice! Don't you realize Prom is the icing on your senior year's cake. It's something you never forget. You remember yours, don't you?

"I didn't go to my Senior Prom," Alice replied.

"Why in heaven not?" asked a shocked Faye.

"I was too busy taking care of my sick mother."

Kelly discretely made her way back to the kitchen to get their spaghetti.

"Oh, Alice, I am SOOO sorry." Faye said. "I feel like such a jerk!"

"It's all in the past Faye. Don't even worry about it. That was a lifetime ago!"

"Still, I am very sorry. That must have been a difficult time for you!"

Alice shrugged. "You do what you have to do. It makes you a stronger person in the end."

"Amen!" added Thelma. "I didn't attend my prom either. I was too focused on entering the Abby and becoming a Nun! Little did I know," she laughed.

Kelly made her way back to the table after the ladies had finished their salads. She quietly began placing their dishes in front of them, not saying a word.

"Hey Kelly," Alice smiled. "We really are interested in hearing what you have planned for this weekend – wardrobe, date and all!"

Kelly smiled back. "You are all very sweet! She began to describe her gown and shoes to the ladies, clutching the empty tray to her chest. And I'm not going to do an "up do". I think they look so cheesy. I'm wearing my hair down with some pretty barrettes to pull it away from my face."

"Sounds just right," agreed Gertie. "I am sure you will be the belle of the ball!"

"So, who is the lucky guy?" asked Faye.

"Adam Lambert!" Kelly smiled dreamily. "We've been dating since our junior year."

"As in Adam Lambert from American Idol?" giggled Faye.

"Lambert?" Alice snapped to attention. "As in Judge Audrey Lambert?"

"No to the first Lambert and yes to the second. That's Adam's first or second Aunt or something. I get all that family tree stuff confused. She's actually the reason that I work here. She recommended me for the job! I better get back to the kitchen or else I'll be looking for another job!" Grabbing their empty salad bowls, she started back to the kitchen.

"So, the old bat actually has a heart," said Alice sprinkling Parmesan on her spaghetti.

"AND she talks!" added Faye, telling the others about their run in with the Judge at Kroger's.

The ladies concentrated on their spaghetti, interspersing light conversation between bites.

Pushing her plate away from her, Alice swallowed and said, "I have a confession to make. I told Lucy about last night."

"You WHAT?" shrieked Faye.

Other diners in their vicinity looked curiously their way.

"You WHAT?" she asked again in a lower tone. "Alice, what were you THINKING?"

"Well, I really had no choice. I forgot to lock up the evidence in my safe last night and invited her to my apartment and well, there it was!"

Thelma crossed herself. "Maybe if I go back to the Abby, I will get dispensation."

"It's all right," Alice assured them. "Lucy just gave me a slap on the hand and made me promise we wouldn't do something like that again. She said she would handle putting everything back."

Gertie leaned back in her chair and gave a sigh of relief. "I don't know how she is going to accomplish that, but she is definitely my new best friend. It looks like our snooping days are over."

"I wouldn't say that" said Alice.

"What are you talking about Alice? A promise is a promise!" said Thelma indignantly.

"I told her 'Scout's Honor.' I was never a Girl Scout!" she said proudly.

CHAPTER SEVENTEEN

After leaving her aunt's apartment, Lucy took the bag of items she confiscated and placed them on the conference room table in the room that was designated for them by William Dunahie. She laced her fingers together and elbows on the table, rested her chin on her hands. What was she going to do with her aunt? She knew she meant well, but sometimes she just went a little too far. Taking the photos out of the envelope, she examined them a little more closely. Yes, Carson James and Jackie definitely looked like a happy couple. When was the last time she had taken a vacation with someone special?

Lucy thought for a while and was shocked when she realized how long it had been. She had been concentrating hard on her career and everything else was put on hold. Was it worth it? Yes, she decided, it was. There would be time enough later to meet Mr. Right. Besides, she smiled, she had Quigley, her little Pug. Dogs were wonderful companions. They loved you unconditionally and demanded very little other than maybe a walk around the block and fresh Kibble.

Putting the pictures back into the envelope, she leaned back in her chair. So, how was she going to get the pictures, file and keys back to where they belonged? She knew Jackie had taken the day off after meeting with her and Lieutenant Sharpe. "No time like the present," she muttered.

Walking to the front desk, she smiled at Robin. Dangling the keys in her hand, she said "Robin, I'm going to take a look at Mr.

James' personnel file. I understand it's in Jackie's office with the others."

Robin pushed up from her desk and smiled. "Of course, Detective Amos. Let me show you where they are."

"No, no problem. I'll just let myself in and then give you the keys back when I'm done."

"Sure Detective. Just let me know if you need anything," she said sitting back down and turning back to her computer.

"Well, that was easy," thought Lucy. Robin never even thought to ask how she had gotten the keys. She probably just assumed that Jackie had given them to her.

Letting herself into Jackie's office, she looked around to see if there was anything that her aunt and her friends may have missed. Taking the envelope with the pictures out of her pocket, she placed them in Jackie's top drawer. Hopefully, Jackie would be too distraught to notice that they were not where she had originally put them. If not, it would just be one of those things that were unexplainable and soon forgotten.

Locking the office behind her, she returned to the front desk, handed Robin the keys and held up the folder. "Got it," she said. "I'll return it after I've had an opportunity to go through it."

Robin glanced at her watch. "I'm going to be heading home now. Do you think you'll be needing me anymore this evening?"

"Just a quick question and then I'll let you go," Lucy replied. "Were you aware that Carson and Jackie were having a relationship?"

Robin blushed and looked down at the floor. "Who told you that?"

"Let's just say I have my sources."

Swiping at a tear trickling down her cheek, Robin looked Lucy in the eye. "Yes, I knew they were having a relationship, but it ended about a month ago, thank God."

"What do you mean by that?"

"Nothing. It's just that Jackie did not deserve Carson James. He was way too good for her. He just finally came to his senses.

That's really all I have to say about the matter."

She picked up her sweater and purse and started towards the door. Turning back to Lucy she said, "Jackie Drake is not all she appears to be. She thinks she has everyone fooled, but she hasn't fooled me! Good night, Detective Amos."

Watching Robin's retreating figure, Lucy said to herself, "Well Aunt Alice, what have you & your friends unearthed?"

CHAPTER EIGHTEEN

With Memorial Day just around the corner, Ken Scranton was busy hanging flags and banners around the facility. The foursome was sitting on the patio watching him.

"Did I tell you that Harry is coming to visit with me Memorial Day weekend?" asked Gertie.

"Oh, Gertie that's wonderful!" smiled Faye. "When is the last time you two saw each other?"

"Believe it or not, it's been since Christmas! I can't believe how quickly the time passes. I am really looking forward to seeing him again. He said he has some "news" to share with me. I wonder if he has finally met a young lady that's acceptable to him. I swear if that man keeps taking his time in settling down, I'll never have any grandchildren!"

"These young people today are so focused on their careers they have totally forgotten about the importance of family," Thelma agreed.

"Christmas?" asked Alice. "Where the heck has he been?"

"Oh, Harry travels quite a bit for his Company. He has been to Thailand and recently got back from China. We talk at least once a week on the phone. I know he feels bad about not getting to see me more often. He knows I'm safe and in good company though." She said smiling at her friends.

Thelma lifted her face to the sunshine. "This feels so doggone good. After the winter we had I thought I'd never feel the sun again."

"We definitely need to enjoy every day," Faye said. "Who would have thought that Mr. James wouldn't be here this year to enjoy such a beautiful day. By the way, Alice, what is Lucy saying about all of this?"

"Hmph! I get to see her about as much as Gertie gets to see Harry and she isn't traveling to any darn foreign country either! And when I DO see her, she's preoccupied with the case. I can't get her to open up about anything!"

"Loose lips sink ships," recited Thelma.

"Hey Ken!" shouted Gertie. "It's almost warm enough for shorts and we'll be able to stare at those sexy legs of yours!"

Ken grinned, waved at the ladies as he hung his last banner and headed towards the front door.

"Ah springtime! Doesn't it make you feel alive?"

Carson James' killer smiled as they watched out the window at the ladies enjoying the day. Yes indeed. Springtime was a time for rebirth and new beginnings. For the first time in a long time, it did feel great to be alive!

CHAPTER NINETEEN

Lieutenant Hector Sharpe entered the conference room juggling a handful of files and a Starbucks cup. Kicking the door shut behind him he addressed his team that had been waiting for his arrival. "Sorry I'm late folks. I had to take a phone call." Taking a sip of coffee, he looked around the room. "Is it just me or is it awfully warm in here?" he asked as he loosened his tie.

"What's the matter Lieutenant? Having a moment? I hear that all day long from my old lady. 'It's too hot in here.' Then, 'where's my sweater, I'm freezing! I swear she's bipolar or something!"

The others in the room laughed as Detective Arnie Fischer mimicked his wife of 30 years.

Fischer had served with the Elmwood P.D. for the last 28 years. He was on the right side of retirement and was looking forward to taking some time with his wife, Louise, and travelling the USA. He partnered with Lucy and had become a surrogate father to her as well as her mentor. She considered him one of her best friends. He reminded her of a giant teddy bear – pleasantly plump but still in good enough shape to keep the bad guys at bay.

Hector Sharpe smiled and put his coffee aside. "I guess I'll start drinking iced tea in the morning and save the coffee for winter. Ok. Carson James. Got the preliminary report from the coroner and just as we expected, he definitely was poisoned."

"Let me guess," ventured Detective Fischer, "arsenic poisoning or antifreeze in his morning coffee."

"Wrong on both accounts Detective. The cause of death is amatoxin toxicity resulting in liver and kidney failure."

"Ouch," said Lucy, "he must have been a world of hurt. What causes amatoxin toxicity Lieutenant?"

"Poison mushrooms!" he replied.

"Where on earth did he get poison mushrooms?" Lucy wondered.

"I guess if we get the answer to that question we'll have our killer," said Detective Fischer.

"I was in that room hours after he was transported," Steve Wilborn, who was the head CSI investigator noted. "Normally I would expect to see some signs of gastric distress like vomiting or signs of diarrhea but unless someone cleaned up after him the office was fairly clean."

"According to the coroners' notes, that probably occurred within 6 to 12 hours after he ingested the mushrooms. He could have attributed it to a bout of influenza because after about 12 hours the symptoms pass and there is a brief period of apparent improvement, but the damage has already been done to the liver and kidneys."

"That's right," Wilborn acknowledged as he entered *amatoxin* into his laptop. "It says here that the deadliest form is the 'Death cap mushroom' or *amanita phalloides* is indigenous to Europe but has since been found in North America – Ohio becoming part of its habitat. 'Amatoxin are cyclopeptides composed of a ring of amino acids that inhibit production of specific proteins within the liver and kidney cells. 60% of the amatoxins travel directly to the liver. Both poisoned and healthy liver cells spit out amatoxins into bile which is then concentrated in the gall bladder. After each meal, the gall bladder releases bile into the gut and the amatoxins travel with salts in the bile. At the end of the small intestine most bile gets reabsorbed back into the liver. Amatoxins re- enter the liver via the same receptors as the bile salts and the poisoning cycle repeats. The other 40% go to the kidneys.' Definitely something you don't want on your Friday night pizza!"

Lucy was thoughtful for a moment. "So how do we know that Carson James didn't ingest these mushrooms accidentally or even if he may have taken them intentionally and committed suicide?"

Fischer grimaced. "If I was going to do myself in, I can think of a thousand less agonizing ways to do it."

"Agreed," nodded Lucy, "so that leaves accidental poisoning or murder."

"There was no trace evidence of mushrooms in his stomach contents so we're not even sure what type of food he ingested that contained them," Rivera continued.

"Well, this is a real conundrum," Wilburn said as he continued scanning his computer. "It looks like there was a case a few years ago in England where a couple added these death cap mushrooms to their Campbell's mushroom soup. She died but he made it. They had no idea the mushrooms were poisonous. Based on the severe reaction you would have after eating even just a minute portion of the mushroom it's not surprising there was nothing left in his stomach. Carson James must have been one sick puppy for a while."

"Are we aware of anything on the menu here at the Manor which could have contained mushrooms within 24 to 48 hours from the day he died?" asked Lucy.

"Now that's a thought worth pursuing," Sharpe nodded. "Amos, can you check with the kitchen staff and check that out?"

"Right away Lieutenant," she replied, and left the room to make a phone call.

Ten minutes later she re-entered the conference room holding a menu in her hand. "Well, I think we have our answer. Chopped sirloin with mushroom gravy, mashed potatoes and corn were the entrée for last Friday evening's dinner. After I talked to the chef, I asked to be connected to Robin at the front desk and asked her if Carson ever ate with the residents. She stated he often had dinner there but would have it brought to his office. She said since he was a bachelor, he used the opportunity so he didn't have to go home and cook for himself. I had her send me a pdf of this month's menu and printed it out."

"Well then why didn't everyone else get sick?" pondered Fischer. "It looks like his dinner was prepared especially for him. We need to determine who had access to his plate prior to him eating it."

"Fischer and Amos, I want both of you to spend some time this afternoon interviewing the chef and his staff, including the waiters. Someone must have some knowledge of how his meal was delivered."

Lucy and Arnie nodded and began gathering up their files as Lieutenant Sharpe pulled a Tootsie Pop out of his pocket and began unwrapping it.

"So how many days has it been?" asked Arnie, referring to Sharpe's attempt to quit smoking.

"Two weeks tomorrow, I'm probably going to need to find a good dentist if I keep eating these damn things. It's the only thing I've found so far that works." Looking at the wrapper he sighed. "Orange. I hate the orange ones," tossing it into the nearest trash can.

Laughing, Lucy and Arnie made their way out of the conference room.

CHAPTER TWENTY

Driving to the Manor, Lucy at the wheel, Arnie asked, "So what are you doing for Memorial Day weekend?"

"I have no plans," she answered. "How about you and Louise?"

"We're having the kids and the grandkids over for a cookout – again!" he muttered.

Lucy smiled. "It sounds like you're ready to hand the gauntlet or should I say spatula and tongs over to one of the kids. You guys always seem to be having everyone over for something."

"It's a real pain in the ass, but you know we wouldn't change it for the world. We love having the family get together. I guess as long as Louise is able to do it, we will but someday, you're right, someone will have to take over the tradition."

"You're so lucky to have such a large family. Mom and James pretty much do their own thing, which is fine, but sometimes it does get a little lonely. Sometimes it's just me and Aunt Alice."

"So how long ago did you dad pass?" asked Arnie.

"Oh geez, I was only 16. Mom was pretty lost for a while but when I went off to college, I was so happy when she met James. She was way too young to spend the rest of her life alone."

"You are more than welcome to come over and have some burgers and dogs with us. There's always room for one more and Louise would love to see you."

"Thanks, I'll keep that in mind but my aunt has been asking me to spend some time with her so I may just join her. Who knows, maybe I'll pick up on some of the gossip from the residents."

"You know Amos, it's ok to take some time off every now and then. You don't always have to be in 'work mode.'"

"I'm not always in work mode – as you call it. I just take advantage of opportunities as they come my way. Ok. Here we are, let's go see what we can find out," she said as she pulled into the Manor's parking lot.

Vincent Lewis was in the kitchen overseeing the preparations for that night's evening meal. The prep table was laid out with small bowls of lettuce and a young man was adding cut up tomatoes and cucumbers to each bowl then covering it with saran wrap. Looking up the young man said, "Hey chef, the cops are back."

Walking up to Lucy and Arnie, he extended his hand. "I'm Chef Lewis, how may I help two f Elmwood's finest?" Lucy firmly shook his hand, receiving a weak, soft handshake in return. "Detective Lucy Amos and this is Detective Arnold Fischer."

Withdrawing his hand and gently rubbing it with his other hand, he sized up the two detectives. "If I'd have known you were coming, I would have cleaned up a bit," he said brushing at an imaginary piece of dirt on his immaculate white coat, then smoothing back his hair in an effected manor. "Are you here to see me or someone else in my kitchen?"

"Actually, we would like to spend a little time talking to each of you."

Holding his hand to his heart, Chef Lewis turned pale. "It's about Mr. James, isn't it?"

"Actually, it is. Is there some place where we can talk with you privately?"

"Yes, of course. Let's go to my office around the corner," he said as he began making his way there in front of the two.

Arnie looked at Lucy and mimicked tinkling a bell. Lucy smiled and began following Vincent Lewis to his office.

Sitting at his desk, he motioned for Lucy and Arnie to take a seat. Nervously smoothing back his hair again, Chef Lewis asked, "Am I a suspect in Carson James' murder? I swear I can't even kill an insect let alone a human being!"

"No sir, you are not a suspect at this time. We are just here to gather as much information as possible about how Carson James received his meals here at the Manor."

"Oh my God!" Lewis squeaked clutching at his heart again, "Do you think my food killed him?"

"Please Mr. Lewis, slow down a little. Again, we just have some general questions we'd like to ask you. No one is accusing you of anything at this point."

"Of course, Detectives," he said folding his hands primly in front of him. "I am here to serve you."

"How long have you worked at Elmwood Manor," asked Lucy taking out a notebook.

"I've been here for the past year. They recruited me from Chez Francois where I was their sous chef at the time. It was an opportunity for me to have my own kitchen, so I jumped at the chance."

"About how many people do you have working under you?" asked Arnie.

"Let me think," he said holding a finger to his forehead and counting to himself. "Between full and part time, I'd say there are about 10 people, including the servers."

"Do you create your own menu, or do you have to prepare certain dishes according to management?"

"Well, I **DO** have creative license to create my own menu, but they do have to be approved by our dietary consultant to make sure our residents are getting well balanced meals. I have been told by her and by management that I am doing a wonderful job.

"I'm sure you do," smiled Arnie. Holding up the copy of the menu Lucy obtained, he glanced down at it and said, "Looks like you put a lot of effort into giving the residents here a variety of meals. I'm impressed."

Chef Lewis smiled at Detective Fischer, smoothed back a stray hair, and thanked him. "So how can I be of help?"

"Last Friday evening you served chopped sirloin with mushroom gravy."

"Yes, I told your assistant that over the phone," he said nodding at Lucy.

As Lucy choked back a response, Arnie quickly said, "Detective Amos and I are co-workers assigned to this case. We were wondering if the mushrooms in the gravy were already added or if you added them yourself?"

"The gravy came that way – with the mushrooms," he responded. "Why do you ask?"

"We were wondering if Mr. James ate dinner at the Manor that evening. If so, it's possible that the meal that Mr. James ingested may have been altered." Lucy said.

"Altered?" Chef Lewis frowned. "What do you mean?"

"It appears that Mr. James died from eating poison mushrooms!"

"Impossible!" sputtered Chef Lewis. "How for heaven sakes could he have gotten poison mushrooms?" he scoffed. "The only mushrooms in my kitchen were already in the gravy."

"So, you don't have any fresh mushrooms hanging around that you may have used or will be using in any other of your dishes?" asked Lucy.

"I purchase all my produce fresh daily. I do not have mushrooms or any other vegetable 'hanging around' my kitchen longer than 24 hours! Maybe he had a pizza from that horrible chain down the street. It would much more likely that he would die from THAT instead of one of MY meals!"

"Again, we're only just speculating at this time," offered Arnie placatingly. "We would like the opportunity to talk to your staff to see if they may have noticed anything unusual that evening. We need to see a schedule of who was working that evening."

"Fine!" huffed Chef Lewis, turning in his chair to his computer screen. Punching a few keys, a schedule came up, he hit print, retrieved the copy from his printer and handed it to Detective Fischer, avoiding eye contact with Lucy. "Let me know when you would like to talk to them, and I will make sure they are available. Now if there is nothing else, I have a meal to prepare."

"Nope, we're good for now," smiled Arnie. "We'll be in touch."

Chef Lewis nodded at the pair and walked out of his office.

"What was that – 'good cop/bad cop'?" asked Lucy. "Oh, that's right. I'm just your 'assistant', the little twit."

Arnie grinned and handed her the schedule. "I'd like 2 copies of this on my desk in the morning. Clear my schedule for the afternoon so we can start interviewing the staff."

"Funny!" shot back Lucy as she showed him her middle finger.

CHAPTER TWENTY-ONE

The Memorial Day weekend arrived with sunshine and temperatures in the 70's. Gertie was putting the finishing touches to her spare bedroom in preparation for her son's arrival when Alice tapped on her door and stuck her head in asking "Is it ok if I come in?"

"Of course!" yelled Gertie from the other room. "I'll be right out."

Alice looked around the apartment, noting fresh cut flowers and the scent of something yummy coming from the kitchen.

"Ta Da!" said Gertie, making a grand entrance into the living room. Her hair had been styled and colored. "What do you think?"

"I think you look fabulous!" smiled Alice. "Harry is going to be bowled over!"

"I can't wait to see him. We have so much to catch up on. I wonder what his news will be?"

"When does he get in?" asked Alice.

Looking at her watch, Gertie replied "1 hour, 20 minutes and 10 seconds."

Alice laughed. "What's that delicious smell?"

"I made a batch of his favorite cookies – snicker doodles!" Gertie held out a platter of cookies to Alice. "Try one."

"If you insist. Oh, my goodness Gertie. These are incredible!"

Gertie put a cup of water in her microwave for Alice's tea and motioned for her to sit down. "This is going to be a wonderful weekend!"

Alice nodded, taking another bite of her cookie. Swallowing, she said "Lucy is coming for tomorrow's picnic too."

"No kidding! That means we can introduce her to Harry!" Handing Alice her cup of hot water, she brought out a variety of tea bags for her to choose.

Alice sighed. "Now Gertie, get the stars out of your eyes. I told you Lucy doesn't have time for romance right now, especially with this murder investigation going on."

"Oh pooh! Everyone has time for romance in their life. We just need to give them a little help!"

Alice laughed. "Gertie you are an incurable romantic. Is there anything I can do to help you before he gets here?"

"No, I think I have everything under control. I'm glad you stopped by before I dust the finish off all my furniture. I can't seem to sit still."

Alice sipped her tea. "Maybe we can pick Lucy's brain about the case. If she's relaxed, she may be more willing to share information."

"Oh, let it go for the weekend Alice. Let's not ruin it by talking about murder and 'who done it?' Let's celebrate the beginning of summer, blue skies and the smell of flowers and fresh mown lawns."

"I suppose," grumbled Alice. "I keep thinking if Lucy can share what she knows it may help me with what's nagging at the back of my brain."

Reaching over and touching Alice's hand, Gertie said "You really do believe you may know something to help this case don't you?"

Alice got up, rinsed her teacup and put it in Gertie's dishwasher. "I don't know. I'm probably being silly. You're right. Let's make it a fun weekend. Enjoy your evening with Harry. I'll see you tomorrow at the picnic."

CHAPTER TWENTY-TWO

"Alice! Lucy! Over here!" Faye shouted waving her arms to attract their attention. She was dressed in red, white, and blue wearing a headband with an American flag.

Lucy and Alice made it over to the table where Faye, Thelma and Gertie were holding chairs for them.

"Happy Memorial Day!" said Faye. "Isn't this something? I think everyone showed up and the weather is perfect!"

Ken Stanton had indeed outdone himself. The banners he had hung the previous weekend were now joined by tables decked out in star spangled tablecloths, red, white, and blue balloons and all of the Manors' residents milling around sipping on drinks and nibbling on appetizers set out at various stations.

"The weather really cooperated this year," agreed Lucy, "and it looks very festive."

Alice looked around and then asked Gertie, "Where is Harry? Don't tell me he didn't make it!"

Gertie grinned. "He's here. He had to make a quick phone call. He'll join us in a minute. He got in right on time and took me out to Café Melissa for dinner. We had a great time! Here he comes now!" she said pointing towards the rear entrance of the facility.

Alice watched as a tall young man dressed in jeans, a plaid dress shirt and sports coat made his way towards them. "I don't remember him being quite so good looking!" she told Gertie.

As Harry reached the table, Gertie grabbed his arm and said "Harry, you remember my friend Alice!"

Harry reached over and gave Alice a hug. "Of course, I do. I don't know what they feed you ladies here, but you all seem to be getting younger and better looking each time I visit."

Harry looked up and saw Lucy standing behind Alice. "You must Lucy. My mom has told me all about you. I understand you will be the future Chief of Police or something like that!"

Lucy laughed. She reached out to shake Harry's hand. "Hi Harry! I've heard a lot about you too. You are quite the world traveler from what I hear!"

"Not anymore!" said Gertie. "Remember I told you Harry had some news to share with me? Well, he has been assigned to a position here in Ohio! No more travelling! Isn't that wonderful?"

Faye and Thelma joined the group handing Alice and Lucy each a glass.

"These are supposed to be strawberry margaritas," said Faye, "but I think you'd have to drink about a dozen of them to get any kind of buzz. Here's to Harry's homecoming!" she said raising her glass. The group raised their glasses, after Harry and Gertie picked theirs up from the table, clinked their cups together and downed the strawberry flavored drink.

The afternoon proceeded without any incidents with the foursome, Lucy and Harry sharing stories and laughing at some of the recent adventures of some of the Elmwood Manor residents. Lucy told Harry about the spaghetti sauce incident and told it in such a way that Harry roared with laughter.

"Who wants another drink? I'm buying," he asked. Everyone raised their hands. "I'll help you get them," smiled Lucy, getting up from the table. The two made their way towards the bar talking amiably and seeming very comfortable with each other.

"I think they like each other, don't you?" asked Gertie.

"Here we go," sighed Alice. "Of course, they like each other. They are both friendly, likeable people. Don't start reading anything into this Gertie."

"Just sayin'...."

"I'm stuffed!" said Thelma rubbing her stomach. "I could have done without that last piece of pecan pie."

"Once again Chef Lewis put together a great picnic," agreed Faye. "His fried chicken was to die for. Oops," she said giggling. "Bad choice of words!"

"I think someone may have had too many margaritas!" noted Thelma.

"Oh please," scoffed Faye. "I'll bet there wasn't even any alcohol in them at all. I'm just having a great afternoon with my 3 best friends!"

Lucy and Harry rejoined the group, handing the ladies their drinks. After finishing hers, Lucy stood up and said, "It has been such a fun afternoon. Thank you for inviting me Aunt Alice. I had a great time, but I need to head out and get ready for tomorrow."

"You work too hard, Lucy," said Alice. "Do you need to go so soon?"

"Yes, unfortunately Arnie Fischer and I have to hold some interviews and I need to prepare my notes. Thanks again for a lovely day," she said, bending over to kiss the top of Alice's head.

"So, we're on for tomorrow evening then?" asked Harry as he stood up to say goodbye.

"Sure, it sounds like fun," smiled Lucy.

"I'll walk you to your car," he said.

After the two were out of hearing range, Gertie whooped with delight "I KNEW it! I KNEW they would like each other!" She grinned broadly at the group.

"You certainly did!" acknowledged Alice, looking in stunned disbelief as her niece and Gertie's son made their way towards the parking lot.

CHAPTER TWENTY-THREE

Lucy let herself into her apartment and was greeted by Quigley at the door. "Hi Buddy! I bet you need to go outside. As she walked Quigley around the block Lucy thought about her day and Harry Smith. "What a nice guy," she thought as she absently waved to one of her neighbors who was taking out her garbage cans to the curb. "Not bad on the eyes either!" recalling his sandy blonde hair, green eyes, and that gorgeous smile. He actually is taller than me too," she smiled. "That doesn't happen very often."

Lucy and Harry had a date to go see the Cleveland Indians play at Progressive Field tomorrow evening. A date! The last time she had a date was that disastrous blind date one of her co-workers arranged with their cousin. It was all she could do to make it through dinner. The conversation was boring (talk about arrogance – enough about me, let's talk about me), and he had to have been no taller than 5'6" tall. At 5'8" Lucy usually seemed to tower over her dates if she wore heels. Thank goodness she had the good sense to have her girlfriend call her cell phone at about 9:30 to fake an emergency, just in case the date was a bust. Believe it or not, she was looking forward to tomorrow evening.

"Steady Amos," she reminded herself. "It's just a baseball game. You have been abstinent way to long..."

Changing into her sweats, Lucy washed her face, moisturized and then sat down in front of her TV with a glass of wine to watch the evening news. She channel surfed for a while and started to doze off as her cell phone went off. Groaning, she hit the send button. "Amos here," she mumbled.

"Lucy?" she heard her aunt's voice on the other end with giggling in the background.

"Hi Aunt Alice, what's up?"

"Honey, we're sorry to bother you but we have a question. How do you re-cork a bottle of champagne?"

"I know I'm going to regret asking this, but why do you want to know?"

"Well, we thought we would end our day having a glass of champagne together. Faye had a bottle in her fridge and since we're all just a little tipsy decided we better save it for another time!" More giggles in the background.......

Lucy smiled. "Unfortunately, you can't re-cork champagne. It won't be any good the next time you want to drink it."

After a moment's silence on the either end, Lucy heard Alice tell her friends "Lucy says we have to finish the bottle tonight. Thank you dear!"

"No! Aunt Alice I didn't say to finish..." but she heard her aunt end the call.

"Thank God none of them are driving," she laughed.

She stretched, turned off the TV and headed for her bedroom. Her cell phone vibrated in her hand again.

"Now what?" she groaned.

"Amos here," she answered.

"Hello Amos, I just wanted to say what a pleasure it was to meet you today and that I am really looking forward to spending more time with you on tomorrow. Is that too forward? If it is, I'm sorry. I'm just a little out of practice when it comes to the dating scene!"

"Harry!" she smiled. "No, you are not being too forward. I had a nice time today talking to you as well and am also looking forward to tomorrow night. By the way, did you know my aunt and your mom and their friends are tying one on as we speak?"

Harry laughed. (She loved his laugh). "How do you know that?"

"I just got a call from Aunt Alice who wanted to know how to re-cork the bottle. I basically told her it wouldn't be the same, so she assumed I said they need to finish it off."

"They'll be fine!" he laughed again. "They'll probably all sleep like babies."

"Aren't you at your mom's?"

"No, I decided to head back to my condo. I love my mother, but there was WAY too much smothering going on there."

"Oh! I didn't realize you already had a home in the area."

"Yeah, when I relocated to Ohio, I bought a condo in Bay Village on the lake. I never really got to use it that much since I traveled so often, so now that I'm back to working out of the office downtown, I can actually start to enjoy it."

"I just assumed since your mom had the guest room ready for you, that you'd be staying with her until you got settled. Lucky you!"

"Lucky me is right! I would stay there when I travelled so we could spend more time together before I had to fly out again. It will be nice to be able to visit and then go home. I love my mother but, well, you know!"

"Indeed, I do!"

"Well, I just wanted to say 'good night' and let you know I'm glad we got to meet!"

"Good night, Harry. I'll see you tomorrow evening!"

Lucy hit end and held the cell phone to her chest. She had butterflies in her stomach. What was that all about? She felt like an adolescent dealing with her first school girl crush.

She went to sleep with a smile on her face.

CHAPTER TWENTY-FOUR

Lucy and Arnie met up in the parking lot of Elmwood Manor the next morning at 8 a.m. Arnie was sitting in his car holding a Starbucks cup in one hand and glazed donut in the other.

Lucy walked over to his car and tapped on the glass. Startled Arnie looked out the window then rolled the glass down.

"I thought Louise had you on a carb free diet?" she asked looking at his donut.

"What she doesn't know won't hurt her," he answered shoving the rest of his donut on his mouth. "The woman is trying to kill me."

"No, I think she's trying to save you from yourself! How was your Memorial Day picnic?"

"Fine. We cooked, we ate, we cleaned up, everyone went home. I thought maybe you'd stop by."

"No, I came here and celebrated with Aunt Alice and the gang. It was actually a good time!" she said smiling.

"What was so nice about it? You spent the day with a bunch of old people!"

"Not all were old," she said coyly. "I met Gertie's son Harry. He's actually very nice!"

Arnie crawled out of his car, brushing crumbs of his suit coat. "Do I detect a little blush there Detective Amos?"

"Don't be silly! I just had a pleasant afternoon with a new friend. So, how are we handling the interviews?" she asked, changing the subject. "Are we tag teaming or doing them individually?"

"There aren't that many working today so let's just do them together."

"Sounds good," she said slinging her bag over her shoulder and heading for the kitchen.

Arnie and Lucy had an opportunity to meet with four of the kitchen staff. Heading back to their cars after about 2 hours, Lucy unlocked her car door and turned to Arnie. "I should have just stayed in bed. What a waste of time!"

"Yeah, really nothing gained. No one really seemed to think there was any way the mushrooms could have come from the kitchen. Maybe we'll have better luck with the afternoon shift. Meet you back here around 2, ok?"

The afternoon shift interviews went pretty much like the morning with no one feeling anything out of the ordinary happened in the kitchen the day before or the day that Carson James died. Everyone agreed that Chef Lewis's kitchen was a well-oiled machine and no one had any reason to harm their Director.

"Other than Chef Lewis, they're basically just a bunch of kids!" Arnie said going through his notes. "High school and college kids working here part time for the most part."

"Maybe he didn't get sick from the food here," replied Lucy running a hand through her hair. "What are we missing? Let's have a team go through the kitchen and take some samples from the pantry and refrigerator just for kicks."

"I'll have Dixon send his people over. That ought to send Chef Lewis into a tizzy! I might come with them just to watch," he laughed.

CHAPTER TWENTY-FIVE

The day following the Memorial Day picnic found the residents of Elmwood Manor gradually returning to their routines. With the presence of the police diminishing, although there was an occasional conversation between residents, it seemed that they felt confident that an arrest was imminent.

Thelma found Alice sitting at the community computer. "There you are. We're going to go work on Big Ben, want to join us?" "I don't think so. I'll catch up with you all a little later." "What are you doing, online Soduko?" "No," said Alice, "I'm actually trying to google information on Carson James."

Thelma sat down next to Alice. "So, are you finding anything interesting?"

"Nothing that we didn't already know from his personnel file," Alice sighed. "I'm starting to think this is going to be one of those unsolved crimes you see on TV."

"It's only been a few days, Alice. Has Lucy told you what's going on?"

"No, as usual she's tight-lipped. You'd think she'd come clean with her own family for heaven sakes."

"Well, I wouldn't take it personally. It's her job. Hey, her big date with Harry is coming up. That's got to make you happy. She works way too hard."

"Yes, she does," Alice agreed logging off the computer. Standing up she linked her arm through Thelma's. "Let's go see if we can finish that darn puzzle."

As Alice and Thelma walked out of the library, Carson James' killer put down the newspaper they were pretending to read and walked over to the computer Alice had been working on. Clicking on the internet history they scrolled through the sites Alice had been visiting. "You don't give up easily do you Ms. Campana? I definitely am going to have to keep my eye on you." Sitting back down, they picked up the newspaper, "Yes, I definitely am going to have to keep my eye on you."

CHAPTER TWENTY-SIX

At five o'clock, Lucy locked up her desk and fairly flew out of the front door of the police station. "Whoa, slow down!" laughed Arnie as he too was heading for his car. "Where's the fire?" he asked innocently. "Just happy it's the end of the day," she answered, slowing her pace.

"Yeah, 'just happy it's the end of the day and that I have a hot date.'" he laughed.

"You don't forget a thing, do you?"

"Hey, I'm a Detective, that's why they pay me the big bucks. Looks like a great night for a game," he said looking up at the cloudless blue sky. "Have a good time, and don't do anything I wouldn't do!"

Lucy shook her head, smiled, and unlocked her car. "This coming from the guy who had five kids!" she shot back. Arnie loosened his tie, sucked in his stomach, and replied, "When you got it, you got it!"

Pulling out of parking lot, Lucy looked in her rearview mirror and waved good-bye to Arnie. Turning on her radio, she started singing along to Ozzy Osborn's "Momma I'm Coming Home," and realized she hadn't felt this excited about anything in a long time.

Walking Quigley, she realized that he was having a hard time keep up with her long strides. Panting and moving his little legs as quickly as he could, he kept looking at her as if to ask her what was going on. "Sorry Quigley," she laughed, "momma's got a hot date tonight!" Scooping the little pug up in her arms she carried him the remainder of the way home, gently placing him on his dog cushion as she undid his leash. "I promise I will walk you two times tomorrow," she apologized as she hurried off to shower. Sighing, Quigley rested his head on his front legs and closed his eyes and fell fast asleep.

Lucy was just spraying some Estee Lauder's "Beautiful" on her neck when she heard the tap on her front door. Taking one more glance in the mirror to check her make-up yelled, "It's open," and headed for the living room just as Harry was coming through the door.

"It's open?" he admonished, shutting the door behind him. "What if I was some sort of perv or serial killer?"

"Then I would have had my killer pug take you down," she laughed, patting the sleeping dog on his head. Opening one eye, Quigley looked at Harry and immediately went back to sleep.

"You look great," Harry said taking in Lucy's Indians t-shirt, jeans and tennis shoes.

"So do you," she said noticing his pressed chinos and dress shirt.

They both laughed. "Either someone is over dressed, or someone is a little too casual," she said.

"My fault," he said. "You can tell I haven't gone to many games."

"Stay right there," she said heading into her bedroom. Coming out she handed him an Indian's jersey. "Try this on." Lucy pointed Harry in the direction of the guest bathroom and waited while he tried on the shirt. Coming out of the bathroom, Harry turned in a circle. "How's this?" he asked innocently. The shirt fit snugly across his chest and shoulders and looked very uncomfortable.

Lucy sighed. "Ok, looks like we go to Plan B," she said ushering him back into the bathroom to put his shirt back on and heading towards her bedroom.

When Lucy came back out to the living room, Harry had changed back into his dress shirt, and she was wearing a yellow summer dress with spaghetti straps and a pair of sandals. Giving each other a "high five" Lucy grabbed her purse, kissed Quigley on the top of his head and locked the door behind her.

CHAPTER TWENTY-SEVEN

By the time the couple got to the game, the Indians were beating the Tigers 2-1 in the second inning.   After buying a couple of hot dogs, a beer for Harry and soda for Lucy, they made it to their seats and soon got caught up in a nail biter with the Tribe pulling ahead in the ninth inning with a 2-run double.   High fiving and cheering with the crowd around them, Harry and Lucy spent the next couple of hours as if they had known each other all their lives. Making their way out of the stadium, Harry grabbed Lucy's hand and headed to the gift shop and purchased some t-shirts and a ball cap for himself.   "For the next game," he told her as the cashier bagged his items. "For the next game," she agreed grinning.

"Want to grab a drink?" Harry asked, again reaching for Lucy's hand.

"I'd like that," she said, giving his hand a little squeeze. "Let's walk over to E 4th street." Turning down Ontario Street, walking along with the exiting fans, they noticed a crowd beginning to form. A group of young men who had apparently had a few too many beers, were shouting at each other, shoving, and throwing punches.   Egging them on, the crowd began shouting, "fight, fight..." laughing and getting caught up in the moment. Lucy and Harry stopped, waiting to see how the situation was going to play out, when one of the young men reached for a gun that he had in his waist band.

Lucy shoved her purse in Harry's hands and sprinted towards

the group, grabbing the young man's arm, twisting it behind his back, forcing him to drop the gun.

"You don't want to do that," she said, pushing him to the ground and placing her knee on his back. A few moments later, 2 policemen made their way through the crowd, relieving Lucy of her perp and ushered him to a waiting police car. "The show's over, folks!" one of the policemen shouted at the crowd. "Hey Detective Amos. Nice job!" the other one said over his shoulder. Lucy smoothed down her dress and headed back to Harry who stood there with his mouth open, holding her purse, while the crowd began to clap. "Thanks Joe," she said. "Lock him up for public intox and menacing with a weapon. I'll come in the morning and file my report."

"Good enough! Thanks for the assist."

Lucy looped her arm through Harry's and said, "How about that drink?"

CHAPTER TWENTY-EIGHT

A couple of hours later, Harry walked Lucy to her door and waited for her to fish her key out of her purse. Before inserting the key in the lock, Lucy turned to face Harry saying, "I can't remember when I have had so much fun. Thank you, Harry."

"You are quite an interesting lady, Lucy Amos. Going to a baseball game has taken on a whole new meaning! I'm not sure how you are going to top this date, but I'd like to do it again soon," he said as he leaned in and kissed her. "I'll call you."

Lucy watched as he made his way down the hallway, feeling like her knees were going to give way before she could open her door. Finally getting her key into the lock, she entered her apartment, locked the door behind her, and sat down heavily on the couch next to Quigley. Quigley rolled onto his back waiting for Lucy to rub his belly. Lucy began rubbing his stomach, then picked him up, hugging him tightly to her chest. "Quigley, I have had the most amazing night! There may be some hope for me after all." Laying him back on the coach, Lucy shut off the lights, got ready for bed, crawled under the covers, grinning from ear to ear as Quigley jumped on the bed, resting his chin on her chest, and both falling into a deep sleep.

CHAPTER TWENTY-NINE

Tuesday morning brought the results from the forensics team that no trace evidence of the poisonous mushrooms had been found in Chef Lewis's kitchen.

"All of the kitchen staff have been interviewed, with the exception of one young lady who was off last weekend attending her high school prom." Arnie noted.

"I'll catch up with her this week," Lucy said, sipping on her iced tea. "I can't see what information a high school student will give us, but we have to cover our bases," she sighed.

"What about the relationship with James and Jackie Drake?" asked Arnie. "Do you believe her story that it ended on a positive note?"

"Who's to say?" asked Lucy. "But I do know that the Administrative Assistant, Robin, isn't a great fan of Jackie's. I think I'll go have a little chat with her today."

"Who's working on the list of locations where these mushrooms can be found?" asked Lucy, placing a check mark on her list.

"Dixon and his team are taking care of that. He said he'd check back with us by week's end."

"How did all the interviews with the residents go? And what interesting tidbits did your Aunt Alice have to add?"

Lucy smiled. "She told us that she remembers seeing Jackie come out of his office after discovering the body, but also that there was someone else 'lurking' in the background, but she can't remember who. We know Jackie discovered the body and we did check out her alibi prior to entering his office. She had just gotten back from an outing with the residents and went in to turn in her payment voucher for gas and found him lying on the floor. My Aunt tends to have a very overactive imagination. As for the other residents, no one saw anything that looked suspicious so basically, a dead end. Pardon the pun."

"This is going to be a tough one to crack based on the fact that he could have ingested those mushrooms just about anywhere," said Arnie scratching his head. "I guess that's what the perp had in mind. I gotta say this is one for the books. We're dealing with someone who definitely thinks outside the box."

"I guess you're not going to tell me how the big date went last night, huh? From what I hear at the station, you may have gone out of your way trying to make an impression. Seriously Amos, can't you ever just go and have a good time and leave work behind?"

"What did you want me to do Arnie? The guy started to pull out a weapon. It wasn't loaded, but how was I to know that? The date did end on a positive note, however," she smiled.

"So, are you going to see him again? Now THAT would be something for the record books. I'm still waiting to hear the list of all the things that are wrong with him."

"The only thing I can think of is he definitely doesn't know how to dress for a ballgame," she laughed and relayed the story of the wardrobe fiasco.

"It sounds like the guy has a great sense of humor. So, I'm guessing the next date will be the one that seals his fate."

Lucy swatted Arnie on the arm with her notebook. "First he has to call me then we'll see."

CHAPTER THIRTY

Robin was putting a file into the cabinet by the front desk and whirled around when she heard Lucy say, "Good morning!" Clutching a folder to her chest she said, "Detective Amos, you startled me!"

"I'm sorry," Lucy said, "I didn't realize you didn't hear me come in. You must have been lost in thought."

Robin dropped into her chair. "I am a little on edge," she admitted. "Are you here to see Mr. Dunahie, I can see if he's busy," she said as she reached for her phone.

"No, actually I'm here to see you. Can you take a few minutes and meet with me in the library?"

"I'll have to see if I can find someone to relieve me. What's this all about?"

"We haven't had a real chance to talk. I want to spend time with everyone who knew Carson James to get a feel for who he was and who may have had a motive to want to kill him."

"I see," said Robin nervously picking at the corner of the folder she was holding. "Let me see if Adam is free."

Ten minutes later Robin and Lucy were sitting at small round table. Robin sat primly with her hands clasped in her lap.

Lucy opened a notebook and began asking Robin questions.

"So how long did you know Carson?" she began.

"Well, I have been an employee here for a little over two years, so I was here when Carson was brought in to replace Mr. Dunahie."

"So, for about a year then," Lucy concluded.

"That sounds about right."

"Tell me a little bit about your relationship with Carson

James."

Robin laughed nervously. "Well, I wouldn't call it a 'relationship.' I am the Receptionist here so my job is to work with the Director ."

"He certainly was easy on the eyes," noted Lucy.

"Yes, Mr. James was good looking. But what does that have to do with his murder?"

"I'm just saying if I had to work with someone that was that sexy, it might make it a little tempting to want to maybe take it to another level...."

"Detective Amos, Carson and I were nothing more than co-workers!" Robin insisted.

"From my understanding, he and Jackie Drake were more than co-workers."

Robin rolled her eyes. "Until he found out what a gold-digger she is."

"How so?"

"As soon as he took the position, you could tell she had her eye on him. If you ask me, she practically threw herself at him. He was a man after all, what did you expect?"

"Tell me how you saw that relationship play out."

"It was sickening. She laughed harder than anyone at his jokes, she pushed him to schmooze with all the corporate higher-ups and was constantly within range. When he was making plans to get away to the Caribbean it was so obvious that she was trying to wrangle an invitation to go along it made me want to vomit."

"So did he ask her to go?"

"Please. When he got back from his vacation and she got back from 'visiting her sick mother' there was no question that they had been together. I've never heard of anyone getting a tan like that in Minnesota in the winter."

"So how long did the relationship last that you were aware of?"

"It was about a month ago when I noticed that she stopped coming by his office and that she looked a little unhappy. She even started losing weight." She sniffed, "it lasted longer than I would have expected but it was inevitable."

"It sounds like you don't have a lot of affection for Jackie."

"She's ok, but women like her are always looking for someone to sweep them off their feet and take care of them for the rest of their life. I have no respect for people like that. You have to make it yourself in this world. So shallow...."

"Did Carson James have any family that you know of?"

"He did mention that he had no brothers or sisters. He said he grew up in Michigan, but that really was about it. I think his parents must have passed on because he never talked about them either."

"When he first came to the Manor, I invited him to have dinner at my place to kind of make him feel welcome, you know," she blushed. "We did have an opportunity to chat a little bit that evening. He went to Michigan State and then to Illinois to get his Master's Degree, I guess that was really the only time we actually had time to really talk."

Robin looked down at her lap. "Is there anything else Detective? I really should get back to work and let Adam get back to his job."

Lucy shut her notebook and stood up. "That's it for now Robin. Thanks for taking time out to talk. If there's anything else I can think of, I'll be in touch."

As Robin walked towards the door, Lucy asked, "Robin is there anyone you can think of that would want to hurt Carson James?"

"Who knows what people are capable of? Sometimes it takes just the littlest thing to throw someone over the edge. I'm sure you see it every day in your line of work," then walked out the door, shutting it softly behind her.

CHAPTER THIRTY-ONE

Lucy decided it was time to sit and have a chat with Jackie Drake. Knocking on her office door she heard her say, "Come in please."

Lucy entered the room and saw Jackie sitting at her desk staring out her office window. Jackie turned in her chair, "Oh, hello Detective Amos. I was wondering when you would make it over to my neck of the woods." She motioned at a chair in front of her desk. "Please, have a seat."

Lucy took a seat and pulled out her notebook. "Jackie the last time we spoke you were obviously very distraught so I thought it may be a good idea to give you some time before we met again."

"No time like the present," Jackie said flippantly.

Lucy looked at Jackie curiously. What a complete turnaround from the weeping, hysterical woman she had talked to just days ago.

Looking at her notes Lucy said, "I know you were the one who found Carson in his office. Would you mind going over the events of that evening again with me please?"

Jackie sighed and moved her chair closer to her desk, folding her hands across her desktop. "As I told you, I had just returned from an outing with the residents, we went to the Natural History Museum to see the Dinosaur Exhibit. I knocked on his door and when no one answered I figured he was out doing something in the building, walked into his office to put the gas receipt on his desk and found him lying on the floor. At first, I thought he was playing around and so I nudged him with my foot and told him to quit being a jerk and to get up. When he didn't move, I knelt by him, felt for a pulse and realized he was dead. I really can't remember what happened next, but I recall running out of his office and heading to the ladies room and throwing up."

"I'm sure it had to have been devastating to find him. I can't even imagine. How would you categorize your relationship with Carson?"

Jackie laughed harshly and said, "Look Detective Amos, let's stop playing games, shall we? I know you know that Carson and I had been involved in a relationship. I found the pictures in my desk, and they weren't where I had put them. I can't believe you had the audacity to snoop in my office without my permission," she said angrily.

Lucy avoided the confrontational attitude and continued to question Jackie. "How long were you and Carson together," she asked softly.

Jackie pulled her hands off of her desk and hugged herself, dropping her hostile attitude and beginning to weep quietly. "Believe it or not, almost from the beginning when he came here. I thought it was love at first sight. He said he felt it too. I really thought he was the one."

Lucy asked, "So what went wrong?"

Jackie stood up and started pacing. "Where shall I begin? Everything was going so perfectly, we even went on that Caribbean vacation as you know from the pictures," she said looking pointedly at Lucy. "I thought he might even propose while we were there. Boy was I ever wrong. He was like a totally different person. He drank too much, flirted with other women, and acted like a complete idiot. He thought he was being funny, but I felt he was offensive and immature. When we got back, I told him I needed some time and do you know what? He didn't even seem like it mattered to him one way or another. I was heartbroken and he acted like it was just another day in the life."

"Jackie," Lucy asked, "were you mad enough to want to hurt Carson?"

Jackie rolled her eyes. "I knew that was coming. No Detective Amos. No matter how much Carson hurt me, I don't have it in me to harm let alone kill another person. You know I have an alibi for that evening anyway."

Lucy looked at Jackie. "Unfortunately, it appears that Carson was poisoned days before his actual death. Did you see any change in him physically at that time?"

Jackie looked at Lucy with a stunned look on her face. "What are you saying? Carson was dying right before my eyes, and I never even noticed it? Oh, dear God," she said dropping into her chair. "So, he really was ill that week. He came in late Monday morning and said he had been vomiting all weekend long and felt like crap. I thought he had just been out drinking and was hung over. Oh, poor Carson! My poor darling Carson!" and started weeping uncontrollably.

Lucy let herself out of Jackie's office. Whatever Jackie felt about Carson, Lucy just didn't get the sense that she was capable of murdering him.

CHAPTER THIRTY-TWO

William Dunahie signed the last check that Robin had left for him to approve, sat back in his chair, and looked around his office. It felt good to be back. Now that all the immediate commotion around Carson James' death had settled down, he was gradually easing back into his old role.

He dialed Jackie's extension but got her voicemail, so he left a message that the payroll checks were ready for distribution. He began cleaning off his desk and logged off his computer when there was a soft tap on his door.

"Enter." He called out and turned to see Lucy Amos walking into the office.

"Detective Amos," he smiled. "To what do I owe this honor?"

Standing up, he reached out to shake her hand.

"How are you Mr. Dunahie?" she smiled. "This won't take long I know you are getting ready to go home."

"Please, take a seat," he said motioning to one of the side chairs, "and please call me William. How is the investigation going?"

"It's progressing. We have a number of leads we are pursuing. We'll be finishing up interviewing the kitchen staff this evening." Pulling a notebook out of her purse, Lucy began leafing through some pages. "I wanted to ask you a couple of questions relating to Chef Lewis and his team."

"Fire away," he said.

Referring to her notes, Lucy asked "How well do you know

Chef Lewis?"

"Well, Vincent has been working at the Manor for about 3 years now. He has done an excellent job and we've had no issues with his work. The residents all seem to like him as do his staff, from what I can see. He takes his job very seriously. Other than that, I really don't know anything about him outside of work."

"How often would you say you take advantage of having your meals here while you are working?"

"Since I've been back, I'd say maybe a handful of times. Why do you ask?"

"When you do eat here, do you go to the dining hall, or do you have the meal sent to you?"

"I call down to the kitchen and he has one of his staff bring me a tray. When I'm done, they come and pick it up. He is very accommodating."

"Are you aware if he ever varies from his menu? By that I mean does he ever create a meal based on a special request?"

"Well, I've never requested a different meal, but that doesn't mean he may not do it. As a matter of fact, I would think he would be more than willing to do so if didn't happen all the time. Like I said, he is very accommodating. Why not ask him?"

"If you requested a food tray to be sent to your office and you were not here when it was delivered, would the tray be left at your desk for your return?"

"Well, of course. They can't be responsible for coming back again if I weren't here. They have left the tray on my desk on a number of occasions. Oh… I see where this is going! Do you think someone came into the office and added something to his food? Who would do something like that?" he said looking alarmed.

"I'm not saying anyone did do that," she said, "I'm just looking at possible opportunities for someone to do so. Mr. Dunahie," she began.

"William," he corrected.

"William," she started again, "I know you were already gone when they hired Carson James, but did you ever meet him?"

Blushing, he began putting his laptop away. "I did have an opportunity to work with Carson to help him transition into his new role. As you may know, I was moved to another position here in the Company based upon some personal issues."

"What was your impression of him based on those interactions?"

"He seemed friendly enough. This was his first time in the role of Director, so he had a lot to learn. Personally, I felt he was a little young to be taking on the job."

"I'm sure it was difficult training someone to take over your position."

He stiffened. "Well, it wasn't the easiest thing that I have ever done, but I swallowed my pride and did what was best for the Manor. Now, if there is nothing else, I have an engagement in an hour. I really have to get going."

Lucy stood up and shook William's hand. "Thanks for your time. I hope you enjoy your evening. I'll let myself out."

William Dunahie stood and watched as Lucy closed the door behind her. "What a fox," he thought. "I'm sure I'll have a wonderful evening," he thought sarcastically as he headed out the door for his A.A. meeting.

CHAPTER THIRTY-THREE

Lucy entered the kitchen at the Manor hoping for an opportunity to interview the final employee on her list.

"May I help you?" one of the kitchen staff asked.

"Yes, can you tell me where I can find, looking at a sheet of paper she found the name she was looking for, Kelly Martin?"

"Sure.   Kelly is over there.   The one with the braided hair," she said pointing towards the time clock. You're lucky. She's just punching out."

"Thanks."

Walking over to the time clock, Lucy gently touched the arm of the young lady who turned quickly in her direction.

"Hi, are you Kelly Martin?"

At the girl's nod Lucy began to introduce herself. "Kelly I'm Detective Lucy Amos with the Elmwood Police Department. Do you have a few minutes to talk?"

"Yes ma'am." Kelly said nervously. "Am I in trouble for something?"

"Not at all," Lucy laughed. "As you probably have heard I have been interviewing all of the kitchen staff about Carson James. It won't take but a few minutes."

"Sure, no problem. Where do you want to talk?"

"It's such a pretty evening, why don't we sit outside at one of the picnic tables.   I'm sure you've been cooped up in here long enough," Lucy said trying to ease Kelly's apprehension in speaking with a police detective.

"Sounds great," Kelly smiled and led the way to the patio outside the kitchen.

"So how long have you worked here Kelly?" Lucy asked taking a notebook from her purse.

"About a year now. I basically work part time some days after school and on weekends. This is my senior year and I'm trying to raise as much money as I can before I head out to Bowling Green this September."

"Bowling Green!" Lucy exclaimed. "That was my alma mater. What a great school and beautiful campus. I'm sure you'll love it there. What do you plan on majoring in?"

"I'm not sure," Kelly said twirling her braid and looking up at the sky. "I thought about teaching but I'm seriously reconsidering.   Sounds pretty dull and boring compared to what you do. Do you like being a Detective?   It must be really exciting!"

Lucy laughed. "Oh yeah, some days I can barely believe my luck!" She caught herself as she realized Kelly was serious. "I do love what I do but there are days where things are very slow, and it feels like you are chasing your tail. When we do break a case, it is the most rewarding feeling in the world – to make a difference- if you know what I mean."

"Absolutely," Kelly said as she stared at Lucy appearing star struck. "Is it hard to become a Detective? I mean, how do I begin to look at getting into law enforcement?"

"I'll tell you what," Lucy said. "Let's get together some day for lunch and we'll talk about it. When I'm done talking, you may just change your mind!" She laughed again.

"Oh my gosh, that would be awesome!" Kelly grinned. "But that's not why you're here today I know. You want to ask me about the day Mr. James died."

"See, you're already on your way to becoming a Detective," Lucy kidded. "Yes, I do have a couple of questions I'd like to ask you."

"One of the things I failed to ask the other staff and Chef Lewis is how far in advance the menu is planned and printed. Would you happen to know that?"

"Sure, that's easy. The menus are printed and posted about two weeks in advance. Meals are very important to the residents here. They all have their favorite meals and look forward to seeing the next time it is going to be served. Let's see," she pondered, "Mr. Stanton loves the liver and onions, Mrs. Kennedy looks forward to spaghetti and meatballs night and your aunt loves our pot roast and potatoes!"

"Oh, so you know Alice Campana is my aunt," Lucy smiled.

"Of course! She is so proud of you. I've heard so many of your stories that she tells her friends when I am waiting on their table. She and Ms. Smith, Ms. Ouellette and Ms. Frank are some of my favorites! They are so funny!"

"Yes indeed, they are quite a foursome," Lucy sighed. "Kelly, can you think of anyone here at the Manor that might have wanted to hurt Mr. James? Did he have any enemies here that you may be aware of?"

"Gosh, not that I can think of," she said in surprise. "All of us girls in the kitchen thought he was pretty dreamy! He always treated us so nice and when we brought him a tray from the kitchen, he always took the time to ask us about our day, school and stuff."

Lucy looked up from her notebook. "How often would you say Mr. James would have a tray brought to his office?"

Kelly thought for a moment. "Well, I can't say for the times that I wasn't here working, but the days that I am here I would say he have us bring him meals a couple of times a week."

"Would you say he mostly did dinner, or did he have breakfast and lunch here as well?"

"Again, I'm usually only here during the dinner hour but I hear he would order his other meals during the day too. Since he was a bachelor, I guess he really wasn't much into cooking for himself. Mr. James' favorite meal was the chef's sirloin and mushroom gravy!"

Lucy tried to hide her excitement. "How do you know that, Kelly?"

Kelly smiled. "Oh, it was common knowledge. When the

menu would come out, he would circle the day and send it to Chef Lewis with a smiley face. We all thought it was funny, but Mr. James had a good sense of humor."

"So, when it was on the menu recently, do you know if he had it delivered to his office that day?"

"Of course," Kelly smiled. "I was the one who brought him the tray. It was the week before prom, and he talked about his own prom when he was a senior. He was Prom King and sounds like he was very popular! He said he was always getting into trouble for the senior pranks he pulled. I bet he was a lot of fun to be around."

"I'll bet he was," Lucy smiled. "Kelly, when you brought him his tray do you know if he ate it right away?"

"Well, that's funny you should ask," said Kelly. "As I was getting ready to go back to the kitchen, he got a phone call about a resident needing something in their apartment fixed. I really didn't pay much attention, but he walked out with me and headed towards the back," she said pointing towards the residents' living quarters.

"Great," Lucy said leaning forward to place her hand on Kelly's arm. "You've been a great help, Kelly. Is there anything else you can recall about that day?"

"No," said Kelly frowning. "Detective Amos, do you think someone came in and poisoned his food? Honestly, I did nothing wrong I swear!"

Lucy straightened up. "Of course, you didn't! Don't even let that thought cross your mind. Now, it's getting late and I'm sure you have things to do. If you can think of anything else, please give me a call, "she said handing Kelly her business card. "My personal cell number is on that so feel free to call me when you want to get together for lunch. My treat!"

Kelly gave her a weak smile. "Thanks. I'll do that!"

Lucy watched Kelly walk over to her car and waved as she slowly drove out of the parking lot.

CHAPTER THIRTY-FOUR

As Lucy drove back to her apartment, she began processing the information that she had learned from Kelly's interview. It was no secret that Carson James would more than likely order the sirloin and mushroom meal that week. It was his favorite. Then what about the unidentified caller interrupting his opportunity to eat it right away. Coincidence? "I think not," she muttered. If his meal was indeed poisoned, the timeline seemed to fall into place based on what Stan Wilborn had discovered about the progression of organ failure after eating the poison mushrooms. Three days after ingesting his meal, Carson James was dead. So, the question is – who wanted Carson James dead and why?

She certainly had something to share at tomorrow morning's briefing. "Note to self," she thought, "never leave any stones unturned." The thought that she had almost decided to forgo Kelly Martin's interview because she was just a "high school student" could have been devastating to the case.

Her cell phone rang, startling her out of her reverie. "Amos," she answered.

"You sound like I caught you in the middle of something," came the voice across the other end.

"Harry! What a nice surprise. Your timing couldn't be more perfect. My poor brain is about to explode!" she laughed.

"Well then, it sounds like you owe me a drink for saving you from the unthinkable," he laughed as well. "I'm on my way back from the office and wondered if you had time to grab a bite somewhere."

"Actually, I am on my way to take Quigley out for a walk. I could meet you some place in about an hour. Would that work?"

"Sounds like a plan. Where do you want to meet and what's the dress code?" he joked.

"Have you been to Hecks yet? They have the best burgers in the world – you have to try their Rocky River burger. It's to die for! Let's sit on the patio. Then we can walk over to Mitchells for ice cream. I will be wearing jeans and a tee shirt so please don't try to out dress me again!" she laughed.

"Jeans and a tee shirt it is! See you about 7:30," he said and hung up.

Lucy tossed her cell phone on her passenger seat grinning from ear to ear. He called again and it felt so natural, like they had been friends forever. "Again, with the butterflies," she said rubbing her belly. Turning on her radio, she turned on the 60's station only to hear Herman's Hermits singing "I'm Into Something Good." "Coincidence? I think not," she smiled.

CHAPTER THIRTY-FIVE

Nine days after Carson James' murder, the residents of Elmwood Manor were gathered in the chapel for a memorial service. Father O'Reilly, the resident chaplain, thought it fitting that there be a sense of "closure" for them and arranged to have the service to allow them to celebrate his life.

It was apparent that people were there for different reasons: to truly mourn his passing or just out of pure curiosity.

Alice and her friends were seated in the 2nd row and watched as an aide pushed Ilse Schreiber in her new wheelchair. Abe, sitting a few seats over looked at the ladies and gave them a wink. Gertie gave him a thumbs up and sat back to wait for the service to begin.

Pictures of Carson James were mounted on poster boards and sat on easels around the chapel. Summer bouquets sat at the foot of the altar and soft music played in the background. The early summer sun shone through the stained-glass windows creating prisms of color throughout the room.

Thelma dabbed at her eyes with a tissue. "He would have been pleased to see how beautiful this is." Faye patted Thelma's arm and nodded in agreement.

Father O'Reilly stepped up to the podium and cleared his throat.

"I would like to thank you all for coming today to celebrate the life of our dear brother, Carson James. He was taken from us much too soon. I thought it only befitting that we take this time to share with each other how he was able to impact all our lives even if it was in some small way. Anyone who wishes to come up to the podium and share their story is welcome to do so. Remember, this is a day of celebration so it's ok to remember Carson with laughter and not just tears.

I thought I would begin with my own story. As many of you know, I am fairly new to Elmwood Manor coming to you from a parish in San Francisco. So, you can only imagine my complete surprise and naivety on how cold Ohio winters can be!" (Laughter in the crowd)

"I came to work one day with the sun shining and no hint of winter in the air, only to leave the building with 4 inches of partly sunny coating my car windshield." (More laughter). "Totally unprepared, I began brushing the snow off my windshield with my bare, ungloved hands only to find a coating of ice underneath the snow. By this time, my hands were numb, my feet were cold and wet, and the darned car door was frozen shut so I was unable to turn it on to begin defrosting my windows. As I was about to head back into the building, Carson was heading towards me with a pair of gloves, hat and an ice scraper and the biggest grin on his face. I remember it well as he began scrapping off my windshield humming "California Dreamin'". Everyone in the room was now grinning, some dabbing at their eyes others outright laughing.

"After about 15 minutes he was able to open my door, start the car and made sure I was ok to drive home. Random acts of kindness which I will never forget and just one example of his caring and compassionate nature. Thank you, Carson,"

"With that being said, please feel free to come up when and if you are ready to speak your piece or take this time to meditate and speak to him in your own way."

Father O' Reilly took a seat in the front row, folded his hands in his lap and sat facing the altar.

An uncomfortable silence pervaded the room for about 5 minutes with no one making a move towards the podium. Finally, Chef Lewis got up from his seat and stood in front of the room. Nervously brushing his hair back, he began to speak. "Some of us in the culinary world come from backgrounds where being a male in the kitchen was thought of as less than macho. My father was embarrassed about my passion and worked long and hard to push me into sports, such as football, where I got my ass kicked (smiles among the room), working on cars where I didn't know a spark plug from a lug wrench, and various other activities that boys should be involved with. The only thing that brought me joy was the ability to make a soufflé that didn't fall or the best tasting pie crust in Lake County. He finally gave up and let me do what I wanted, but the bond was forever severed and my self-esteem as a boy was shattered. Although I continued to do what I loved, there was always that self-doubt in the back of my mind about my self-worth. As a result, I stayed in the background in all my jobs. Always a sous chef, never a chef!" he laughed. When the position for head chef was posted here at Elmwood Manor, I decided to take a chance and apply for the job, already believing it would be another dead end. That is when I met Carson James and actually found someone who decided to take a chance on me and got the position. I will be forever indebted to Carson for giving me this opportunity and the ability to gain a new family who loves me for who I am." Wiping a tear from his eye, he looked down at the ground and headed back to his seat. Someone in the room began clapping and within moments the chapel echoed with applause.

For the next hour, residents took turns either standing up and telling their story, some making it up to the podium, but it was an hour of bonding and coming together as a community.

As everyone made their way out of the chapel, Thelma stopped and gave Father O'Reilly a hug. "Thank you, Father," she said, "we all needed this," then made her way back to her room to be alone and meditate.

Carson James' killer watched as the crowd dispersed. "What a bunch of crap. Perhaps you should have heard MY story about Carson James," and headed down the hallway.

CHAPTER THIRTY-SIX

Lucy sat waiting for the morning briefing to begin. Sipping on her Star Bucks she saw Arnie walk into the room and motioned for him to join him, reaching under her seat to hand him another coffee she had purchased for him. Raising his eyebrows, Arnie said "Someone woke up in a good mood. Thanks for the coffee, but what's the occasion?"

"I'm just happy to be alive and wanted to spread the love." She grinned.

Overhearing their conversation, one of the other cops said out loud "Hey everyone, I think Amos got laid last night." Everyone laughed and broke into cheers.

Lucy blushed and said "Really? How old are you guys? Can't someone just be happy without sex being involved?"

"NO!" several them shouted and more laughter erupted.

Lieutenant Sharpe entered the room, iced tea in hand, and said, "Well I'm glad you're all in such a great mood because we have a full day ahead of us." Groans came from throughout the room. Sharpe went through the items needing attention for the day, with most of them heading to their respective squad cars after the meeting. Lucy, Arnie, and the rest of the Detectives stayed behind to update him on their ongoing cases.

"Ferguson and Miller nice job on tying up the Henderson case," Sharpe said looking at his notes.

"Long time coming, Lieutenant," Joe Miller said, "but we finally got the old lady to crack and realize what a whack job her grandson really is. He'll be going to trial in a couple of weeks."

Sharpe nodded and looked at Lucy and Arnie. "What do we have new on the James murder? Tell me we're making progress.

I'm starting to get some pressure from City Hall. Doesn't look good to have an unsolved murder in the city, blah, blah, blah."

Arnie spoke first, "This is a tough one. So many people had an opportunity but so far we just can't figure out the motive."

Lucy looked at her notes. "I spoke with one of the kitchen staff yesterday, Kelly Martin, a high school girl who works part time. She was able to give me some interesting tidbits." Lucy then went on to relay Carson's affinity for the mushroom sirloin meal at the Manor, the interruption of his meal by the phone call, giving someone an opportunity to poison the meal and his reputation as a prankster in school. "It certainly backs up our theory on the how and the when, we just need to figure out the who and why."

Lt. Sharpe sighed. "Let's do a deep dive in Mr. James' reputation both in high school and college. Maybe we're missing the big picture on just who this guy really was."

Lucy and Arnie began packing up their things and were headed out the door when Lucy turned and said, "I guess there is a memorial service for Carson today where he will be eulogized by the residents. You're right, maybe we need to find out exactly who Carson James was. I'll stop by and talk to my Aunt Alice to find out how it went."

CHAPTER THIRTY-SEVEN

Lunch at the Manor was more somber than usual with residents talking quietly among themselves at their tables.

"It really was a beautiful ceremony," Thelma said using her napkin to wipe tomato soup from her chin.

"Do we know what they did with his body?" Faye asked.

"Lucy said they sent his ashes to someone in Michigan who was the Executor of his Estate," Alice said. "That's all I know. I guess he had a will and wanted to be cremated. That's the way I want to go out. I don't want everyone standing over me and saying, 'how good I look.' How good can you look when you're dead!"

"Do you know how the tradition of sending flowers to a funeral got started?" asked Gertie. "Before people started sending the corpses to a funeral home, as we all know, family members were laid out in the parlor prior to getting buried. After a few days the bodies started smelling a little ripe, so people would have flowers around the casket to mask the smell."

"Gertie you are always so full of interesting information," Faye said admiringly.

"And I don't want anyone sending flowers," Alice continued as if she hadn't been interrupted. "What a waste of money! I'm going to have everyone donate to their favorite charity in remembrance of me!" she finished with a satisfied nod.

"I wonder if anyone had a funeral for Mr. James?" asked Faye. "I don't think he had any immediate family. How sad!"

"Which is why our little memorial service was perfect," Thelma said. "There were some pretty interesting stories, wouldn't you say?"

"Yeah, he sounded like a real saint!" Alice retorted. "No one can be that perfect. Did you notice Jackie didn't speak up?"

"There were a lot of people who didn't Alice," Faye said reprovingly. "That doesn't mean anything. She may have been too emotional to say anything."

"Or too guilty," added Alice.

"Well look who just walked in," smiled Gertie as she waved at Lucy who was just entering the dining hall. "Lucy, over here," she said waving her arms.

Lucy smiled at the group and pulled an empty chair from a neighboring table and sat down with the foursome.

"How are my four favorite Elmwood Manor residents?" she smiled.

"Happy to be alive!" Thelma chimed in. "We were just talking about the memorial service Father O'Brien had for Carson. It was getting a little maudlin so we're happy for the interruption."

"Sorry I missed it. Tell me all about it if you don't mind."

The group took turns relaying stories that residents and staff had shared about their experiences with Carson James. Lucy smiled at Father O'Brien's story and felt a little ashamed for her treatment of Chef Lewis after hearing about his childhood.

"So, no one had anything negative to share?" she asked the group.

"Oh, heavens no!" exclaimed Faye. "That would have been totally inappropriate!"

"Of course," agreed Lucy. "Sorry, it just crossed my mind that no one is that perfect so I'm sure there were things unsaid. It would be interesting to hear about that side of Carson James as well."

"That's exactly what I said!" Alice said triumphantly. "I'm sure Jackie Drake could have shed some light!"

"Don't speak badly about the dead," said Thelma crossing herself.

"Well, I think it was a nice gesture on Father O'Brien's part to set the service up," said Lucy rising from her chair.

"Where are you going?" asked Alice. "Stay and have a grilled cheese and tomato soup," she said motioning to a server to come to their table. "What do you want to drink? We gave you our information, so it's time to give us some. Tell us what's going on with the case!"

Lucy sat back down and agreed to have some lunch with the ladies. While waiting for her grilled cheese and soup to be served she shared what she could about the ongoing investigation.

Alice sighed, "So there's really nothing new is what you're saying…"

"All in good time Aunt Alice. As you know there is a lot of moving parts that need to be examined."

"Enough of all this depressing stuff," said Gertie leaning forward in her chair. "Tell us about how things are progressing with you and Harry!"

"Oh, didn't you hear about the upcoming nuptials?" Alice asked sarcastically. "Good grief Gertie, they've known each other not even a couple of weeks. What do you mean 'progressing'? Geez……"

Lucy smiled. "Harry and I had a great time at the Indians game and met up again for dinner last night at Hecks. He is very sweet," she said looking at Gertie.

Alice looked stunned. "You've seen him twice already? Boy he's a fast mover."

Gertie turned and gave Alice a glare. "What do you mean by that?"

Alice looked back at Gertie. "What I mean is he sure doesn't waste any time trying to get into my niece's pants!"

"Aunt Alice!" Lucy said laughing. "Oh my gosh, I can't believe you just said that. Harry has been a perfect gentleman. Stop that!"

Gertie got up throwing her napkin on the table. "If you'll excuse me ladies, I think I'll go lie down for a little while. It's been a long morning."

Watching Gertie's retreating figure, Lucy said "I think you may owe Gertie an apology Aunt Alice."

"Hmph," said Alice looking a little uncomfortable. "She'll get over it. She just needs a nap."

With that the group all rose from the table, said their good-byes to Lucy and headed back to their separate apartments. As Lucy was leaving the room, the waiter handed her a takeout box and container for her soup and sandwich.

"I was getting ready to give you this, but things sounded like they were getting a little heated at your table," he said.

"Thanks!" Lucy said, taking the bag. "Never a dull moment here!"

He laughed, nodded in agreement, and headed back to the kitchen.

CHAPTER THIRTY-EIGHT

Arnie and Lucy met up at the station to begin delving into Carson James' background.

Pulling the personnel file that she had gotten from her Aunt Alice, she hesitated as to whether she would tell Arnie the story of their caper. "No," she thought, "better keep this one to myself."

Spreading the papers out on the desk they started looking at his resume.

"OK," said Arnie as he looked at the document from an outstretched arm.

Lucy started laughing. "Arnie, when are you going to admit that you need glasses - when your arm isn't long enough anymore?"

"Very funny Amos. As a matter of fact, Louise bought me some readers but I'm not ready to concede yet. I look like a Poindexter in them."

"And they call WOMEN vain! For heaven sakes break them out and let's get on with this."

Sheepishly Arnie pulled an eyeglass case from the pocket of his sports coat, opened the case, and put them on. "Don't you dare say a word!" he muttered.

Lucy looked him over. "As a matter of fact, they make you look distinguished! I like the look. Seriously."

"You had me until you added 'seriously'. That just means you're trying to convince me and don't mean it."

"Oh Lord," Lucy said slapping her forehead. "You really are too much! I like the look and if they help, who the hell cares what anyone else thinks? Arnie you are such a jerk!"

"Love you too Amos," he said. "Actually, they do help so what the heck? Another victory for the aging process!"

Picking up the resume again Arnie continued to speak, "Bachelor of Science in Business Administration from the University of Michigan and then he got his MBA from the University of Chicago graduating cum laude. Not a bad resume. He was a pretty smart guy apparently."

"Member of Pi Kappa Alpha fraternity at U of M, Toastmasters Club and National Honor Society, lettered in golf and track," continued Lucy. "Sounds like a well-rounded individual."

"So, where do we start?" asked Arnie. "The guy didn't have any family to speak of so who do we talk to?"

"How about the Executor of his Estate?" Lucy suggested. Do you have the name and number?"

Pulling a copy of Carson's will from his file, he said "Guy's name is Trevor Rathbun. Man, I'm picturing hoity toity country club, silver spoon in his mouth, high class pedigree just hearing the name."

Lucy rolled her eyes. "Want me to make the call?" she asked.

"Yeah," he said writing the number on an index card. "I don't deal well with the upper class. I'm too guttural."

"How does Louise deal with you every day? The woman deserves a medal."

"I'm the best thing that ever happened to her, just ask her!" he said looking offended.

"Yeah, I'll make sure I do that the next time I see her."

CHAPTER THIRTY-NINE

Lucy pulled her cell phone out of her purse and dialed Trevor Rathbun's number.

"Hello, you've reached the voicemail of Trevor Rathbun with Madison, Hildebrand and Turner. I'm either on another line or with a client but leave your information and I will return your call as promptly as possible."

"Mr. Rathbun, this is Lucy Amos, Detective with the Elmwood Police Department here in Ohio. I would like to talk to you about Carson James when you have a moment. Please call me at your earliest convenience, although sooner rather than later would be appreciated as we are in the middle of investigating his murder. Thanks, and hope to hear from you soon."

Hitting the end button on her phone, Lucy looked at Arnie. "Hopefully Mr. Rathbun gets back to us quickly. I feel we're kind of at a dead end right now."

Arnie was looking at his notes. "Did we ever hear back from Steve about where the mushrooms can be found?"

"No, come to think of it. Do you want to give him a call or should I?"

"I'll call and see what interesting tidbits he has to share. I need a bottled water any way. Maybe I'll stop by his office and see if he's in. Want anything to drink?"

"No," said Lucy as her cell phone began to ring.

"Lucy Amos," she said giving Arnie a thumbs up, mouthing 'Trevor Rathbun' as she listened to the voice on the other end.

Arnie nodded and headed out the door to speak to Steve Wilborn.

"Detective Amos," Trevor said. "I'm glad you called. I was planning on getting in touch with you as well, so your timing is perfect. I figured you might want to speak to me. Things have been a little hectic here as you can imagine. I plan on coming to Elmwood in the next day or two to tie up some loose ends and pack up Carson's belongings. Would you be interested in meeting at his condo on Friday? It may be easier than trying to do this over the phone, I'm in between meetings and pressed for time today."

"I'd appreciate that Mr. Rathbun. I do have a few questions, but they can certainly wait until then."

"Fantastic. Let's say we meet around 1:00? Do you need the address?"

"One o'clock is fine. I have his address here in my file."

"Ok then. I have you added to my calendar. Unless I hear from you otherwise, I will see you on Friday. Talk to you then," he said ending the call.

"Well, that was short and sweet," she thought putting her cell phone on the table. A couple more days wouldn't make or break the case, plus she preferred interviewing people in person, so it was an ideal situation that he had to come to town.

"Might as well make use of my time and prepare what questions I want to ask him," she decided as she pulled out a fresh sheet of paper from her tablet.

Fifteen minutes later, Arnie came back into the room sipping on a bottled water. He placed another bottle next to Lucy. "Don't say I never gave you anything."

"Thanks."

"How did the phone call with Trevor Rathbun go," he mimicked using his worst Robin Leach accent.

"Short and sweet. He's coming to town this weekend so we're meeting with him at 1:00 at Carson's condo on Friday. He's planning on making arrangements to have his belongings packed up and closing the condo down. We should have his undivided attention."

"Sounds like a plan," Arnie said taking a last gulp of his water and tossing the empty bottle towards a trash can. "Three points!" he said as he hit it dead center in the receptacle.

"What did Steve and his team have to say about the mushrooms?"

"Believe it or not, the darn things grow in Avon Lake right in Elmwood's back yard practically. Back in 2012 about a dozen people ate some in a chicken cacciatore someone made and became deathly ill. No fatalities luckily but some serious liver damage occurred in a few. I guess they were treated at University Hospital. It made the news on TV 8 as well as some local newspapers. Boiling, cooking, or even freezing them doesn't kill the toxins. I guess they taste pretty good but the aftereffects are usually deadly or at the least causes hepatitis or liver damage. Nasty stuff. They originated in Europe but arrived on the roots of imported ornamental trees around 1938 in California. Now, seven decades later they have adapted and grow in many states including Ohio."

"I wonder why Carson James wasn't lucky enough to survive?" Lucy pondered.

"Steve said that staying hydrated can prevent death. If Carson was as sick as he told Jackie he was, then more than likely he was pretty dehydrated which speeds up the process. According to the autopsy report, his kidneys had totally shut down."

"I never even heard of them until this case," said Lucy. "Obviously someone was paying attention to the news," she shuddered. "No more mushrooms on this girl's pizza from now on!"

"On that note, I am packing up and going home to hug Louise and the kids! See you tomorrow!"

CHAPTER FORTY

Alice sat in her apartment sipping a cup of tea. What was going on with Lucy? She had always been so focused on her career and now all she was thinking about was Harry Smith! Gertie needed to mind her own business and stop pushing so hard to get the two together!

A tap on the door interrupted her thoughts. Looking through the peephole she saw Faye standing in the hallway.

Opening her door, she motioned for Faye to come in.

"I was just having a cup of tea; would you like one?"

"Sure, that would be nice, thanks."

"Go ahead," Alice said as she put the kettle on to boil. "Tell me what a schmuck I am."

Sitting herself at the table, Faye slowly shook her head. "I just wanted to stop by and see if you're ok. You haven't been yourself lately. I thought you might want to talk."

"There's nothing to talk about. We've got a killer wandering around the Manor, the staff all look at each other suspiciously, Lucy's got herself a new boyfriend, my sister is never around for either me or Lucy but other than that everything is just peachy!"

Alice busied herself putting out a cup and saucer, tea bags and cream and sugar, avoiding looking at Faye.

Faye paused for a moment before speaking. "When I got the phone call that Scott was hurt at the plant, I remember time standing still for a moment. I honestly don't even recall how I made it to the hospital, but somehow, I had made arrangements for someone to come stay with the kids and drove myself to the ER safely. Unfortunately, I got there too late and Scott had already passed. I didn't even get say good-bye to my best friend and love of my life." Tears trickled down Faye's cheeks. "All I kept thinking was 'what am I going to do now, what am I going to do now?' I had no job, I had 3 young children depending on me and all my family were living in another state. I felt so alone, and the sadness was unbearable."

Alice handed Faye a couple of napkins and sat down next to her, taking her hand.

"But you know what Alice? I survived. I survived and my children survived. So why am I telling this to you? Because we all have peaks and valleys in our lives and how we navigate those peaks and valleys is what determines the next chapter in our lives. I'm sorry I'm not doing this very well."

Alice shook her head. "No Faye you are making a lot of sense."

Blowing her nose Faye continued. "I was lucky enough to have a very dear friend who came to my rescue. We spent many nights with her either coming over to sit with me or taking a phone call from me at 3 in the morning. She was the wisest woman I have ever known. Do you know what she told me Alice? She told me to count my blessings! My world had just fallen apart, and she was telling me to count my blessings! How could that possibly be?"

The tea kettle started whistling so Alice got up and poured the hot water in a mug and handed it to Faye.

"Every night and every morning my job was to go through a list of things I was grateful for. At first, I struggled to find one thing I was in such despair. But pretty soon my list of 2 or 3 started growing and before you knew it, I was able to look beyond the despair and find some rays of hope. Sounds corny huh?"

"Not at all," Alice said as she sat back down at the table. Your friend was absolutely right. We get so caught up in what is wrong in our lives we forget all the good things we should be thankful for. I know where you're going with this Faye."

"Look Alice, I'm not trying to be "preachy" or anything, but in some small way I see you heading down that path and now it's my turn to help- if you'll let me of course!"

"You already have. I have been a schmuck. Lucy has always been like my own daughter. Jane is a good mom, don't get me wrong, but sometimes I think her priorities aren't always right. Lucy and I have become very close over the years. I think I'm feeling a little worried that if she finds someone to love, she'll forget about me. Selfish huh?"

"A little," Faye agreed "but it's just human nature to protect what we think belongs to us."

"Ouch," said Alice. "You could have sugar coated it a little!" she laughed. "But that's not what I need right now I know. Thanks Faye, you are a good friend. It's time for me to stop having my pity party and start focusing on what I have to be thankful for as well."

"An attitude of gratitude," Faye quoted.

"You've been around Thelma too much!" Alice smiled.

"Well, she is definitely on my list of people and things to be grateful for," Faye said.

"Me too," Alice agreed. "Now I am going to kick you out because I have something I need to do. Gertie deserves an apology and there's no time like the present."

Hugging Faye, Alice let her out of the apartment, gave a collective sigh and headed towards Gertie's apartment to make things right again.

CHAPTER FORTY-ONE

At exactly 1:00 p.m. Lucy and Artie pulled into the driveway of Carson James' condo. A pearlescent white Denali was sitting in the open garage with Michigan license plates. As they walked towards the front door it swung open and a heavy-set man with a receding hairline, wearing jeans and a flannel shirt with the sleeves rolled up smiled at them, looked at his watch and said, "Impressive. Right on the dot. I love it when people are punctual. Trevor Rathbun," he said reaching out to shake their hands. "Come on in but forgive the mess. I've got to say I'm a little bit out of my element here and don't even know where to begin."

Half packed boxes were scattered around the condo. Lucy took in the furnishings. Leather couch, 52" plasma television, marble fireplace with a piece of art she recognized but couldn't place caught her eye. Arnie whistled. "Nice set up!"

Looking around Trevor agreed. "Carson liked nice stuff that's for sure. Now the question is what do I do with it all? Have a seat," he motioned to the leather sofa. "I have some bottled water or a beer if you're interested."

"Water would be great," Lucy said.

Trevor handed them each a bottle and sat down on a matching leather recliner. He sighed and put the footrest up, wiggling his feet in socks with holes on the bottom. "I got in last night and thought I would be out of here by the end of the day." He laughed and looked around. "That's not going to happen."

Arnie agreed. "Looks like you have your hands full. We're not going to take up a lot of your time but would really appreciate it if you can shed some light on who Carson James was."

Lucy asked, "Tell me a little bit about how you knew Carson and your relationship."

Trevor took a swig from a beer bottle and answered "Carson and I go way back. We were fraternity brothers at the U of M. Pi Kappa Alpha fraternity. Seems like a lifetime ago. God we were so young and naïve. We met our sophomore year during rush, both pledged and ended up being roommates until we graduated."

Getting up from the recliner, he went to a box and pulled out a yearbook. Opening to two dog eared pages he showed them picture of himself and Carson. Look at those baby faces. Not to mention I was about 50 pounds thinner," he laughed, rubbing his protruding belly. "Ten years of sitting behind a desk and pouring over law books has certainly taken its toll."

Trevor showed them some other pictures of himself in a football uniform, track uniform and prom court pictures.

"So, you played a little ball," noted Arnie. "What position did you play?"

"Halfback!" Trevor said proudly. "Wasn't too bad either, if I say so myself."

The two chatted for a while about U of M's current record and their thoughts about making it to Outback Bowl this year.

"What kind of law do you practice?" asked Arnie circling back to his questions.

"Criminal law. I'm a defense attorney. How ironic what with Carson being murdered. How is the case going? Are you getting close to making an arrest – not that I would represent the scumbag that did this! Man, I still can't believe he is dead!"

Looking through the yearbook that Trevor had given them, Lucy asked "Is it ok if I keep this for a while?"

"Sure. Do what you want with it. I have one at home somewhere. One less thing I have to pack."

"In answer to your question," Lucy said "we are making some progress in figuring out how Carson died but at this point haven't figured out the who or the why. That's why we thought it might be helpful to get a handle on Carson's past and any bearing that could possibly have."

"Got it," he said taking another swig from the bottle. Getting up to get another from the refrigerator he kept talking. "Carson was a lot of fun to be around - very personable and smart. Man, that guy could pull an all-nighter and still ace his exams the next day. One of those guys who could read something once and retain it. Lucky bastard. The rest of us spent hours at the library trying to maintain a 3.0 and he was out escorting out the sorority chicks to their events and getting laid weekly. Sorry," he said looking at Lucy.

"I'm around cops and detectives all day long," she said, "trust me, I've heard it all!"

"Are you aware of any other fraternity brothers or college friends he may have stayed in touch with?" asked Arnie.

"Probably not. Carson was fun but he held people at arm's length. I never knew him to get close to anyone other than me. All his friendships were kind of superficial. I'm not sure how I won the lottery to be his best friend, but it worked for both of us."

"What about family?" Lucy asked. "From what we can see, it doesn't appear he has any."

"Now that is a sad story. When Carson was a senior in high school his mom, dad and brother were involved in a horrific car accident. They got t-boned by a semi who ran a red light. No one made it. I guess he was a star athlete at the high school and an honors student, so I really think he buried his grief in focusing on school. He got a full boat scholarship. He said he stayed with some friends of his folks until he graduated and never looked back. I'm not too sure about grandparents or any other blood relatives. He was pretty private in that respect. I don't claim to know a lot about psychology, but it was apparent he put up a good front but there was a lot of pain behind it. I remember one summer I invited him to spend some time at our family's country estate in the Hamptons."

Arnie glanced at Lucy as if to say, "I told you so."

"One morning I got up and looked out my window and saw

Carson sitting on the dock staring out at the water. I walked down to sit with him, and you could tell he had been crying. Once he saw me, he started clowning around and pushed me in the lake and jumped in after me. I think that was the only time I ever saw him let down his guard."

"Can you think of anyone who would want to hurt Carson?" Arnie asked.

"God no! Carson was a prankster and sometimes he took it a little too far, but as far as I know everyone liked the guy."

"So how were you lucky enough to be Executor of his Estate?" asked Lucy.

"When Carson was in grad school, he called me one night and said he was taking a class, financial planning or something like that and the professor suggested they all get their affairs in order, like getting good disability insurance, making living wills and stuff that most college kids don't even begin to think about. Carson was impressed with the guy and appreciated the fact that the professor made them think about their own destinies. He asked if I would consider being the Executor of his will as he considered me his only family. Of course, I said yes, never knowing that I would be fulfilling that task so soon."

Arnie and Lucy both stood up. Shaking Trevor's hand Arnie thanked him for taking the time to meet with them. He and Lucy both handed him their business cards.

Trevor took the cards. "It was nice to meet you both. I wish you all the best in catching the bastard that did this. I'll call you if I think of anything else and I hope you'll do the same."

He sighed, looking around the condo.

"You know," said Lucy taking in the mess, "there are a lot of charitable organizations like Habitat, Salvation Army or the Veterans who would be happy to take his belongings. I hear they will even come and box them up for you and haul them away."

Trevor brightened at the thought. "What a great idea! I'll start making some calls right away. Thanks a lot!"

Giving a final wave, he shut the door behind him.

"Helluva nice guy," Arnie said as he got behind the steering wheel.

CHAPTER FORTY-TWO

After Arnie dropped Lucy off at the station, she got into her own car and headed over to Elmwood Manor. Her Aunt Alice's behavior the day before was bothering her so she decided to pay her a visit.

Robin looked up from some paperwork she was doing when Lucy came through the front door.

"Hello Detective Amos," she said brightly. "Are you here on business?"

"No, I just thought I would stop by and say hello to my aunt. Have you seen her lately?"

"I think they are working on their Big Ben puzzle she said pointing down the hallway," and went back to her work.

Lucy found the four friends cheerily talking and trying to fit pieces in the half-finished puzzle. She was relieved to see that Alice and Gertie were working side by side with no evidence of any bad feelings.

"Lucy! What a nice surprise," Gertie said as she put a piece into the puzzle and patted it into place.

"Hi everyone," she said as she walked over and gave her aunt a kiss on the cheek. "Well, I give you one for your tenacity she said looking at the puzzle."

Faye laughed. "It's a real bitch!" she said and clapped her hand to her mouth.

Everyone started laughing. "Faye Ouellette, that is the 2nd time in as many weeks that I have heard you swear," laughed

Alice. "It's nice to see you let your hair down."

Faye grinned. "My kids are going to take me out of here with you all being such bad influences on me!"

"We're just killing time until dinner," Alice said. "Can you stay and have dinner with us?"

"Harry is coming to eat with me," Gertie said and looked quickly at Alice.

"Let me know if you can stay and I'll go let the kitchen know," Alice said graciously smiling at Gertie. "I'm sure Harry would love to see you."

Surprised at the change of attitude, she said "Sure, I'd love to stay."

Alice left the room to let the staff know to set another place.

Gertie looped her arm through Lucy's and walked over to a sofa. "Your Aunt and I had a little chat. It seems she is afraid of losing you to Harry."

"Oh, my goodness," said Lucy in surprise. "What a silly idea!"

"I basically told her the same thing and I think she is coming to terms with the idea that you may actually be interested in a something other than your job. She apologized and all is well!"

Lucy spent the next half hour with the group trying to find a piece that would fit without any luck. "I give up she said," tossing a piece she had tried in at least 10 different spots back onto the table.

"I thought I recognized that voice," said Harry peeking his head into the room. "Hi Lucy!" he said and gave her a quick hug. The ladies exchanged quick glances, and Gertie hid a grin behind her hand.

"Looks like we're all dining together," she said blushing.

Thelma looked at her watch. "Let's head on down there now so we can get served first."

The party of six got settled at their table and chatted casually until the server, Kelly, came to take their order and headed back to the kitchen.

Lucy told them a little about her visit to Carson James' condo.

"Harry, didn't you tell me you were a Pi Kappa Alpha at Cincinnati?" Lucy asked.

"Oh yes," Gertie chimed in. "We heard quite a few stories of his escapades with his brothers down there!"

"Small world, but Carson James was also Pike at the University of Michigan. As a matter of fact, I have a copy of his yearbook where it shows a picture of him with his fraternity brothers. Let me go grab it for kicks."

Kelly came by the table with their drinks and Lucy headed to her car to get the yearbook.

While waiting for their meals to be served the group took turns looking at the book commenting on how young Carson was but still being able to see the similarity in the man he had become.

Kelly appeared with their salads and saw the book. "Hey, I've seen that book before," she said setting their plates in front of them.

"Oh, in Carson James' office?" asked Lucy as she started pouring dressing on her salad.

Kelly paused. "No that's not where I saw it. I can't remember where, but it wasn't in his office. It'll come to me." Shrugging she walked over to the next table to take their order.

Reaching for the pepper, Alice knocked over her glass of water. Harry and Lucy sprang into action using their napkins to soak up the water while everyone scooted away from the table to avoid getting wet. One of the other servers came over with some towels and wiped up the remaining water, replaced their tablecloth, dinner resumed and the yearbook was tucked away in Lucy's bag and forgotten.

Observing the yearbook being passed around the group's table, a shaken killer excused themself and left the dining hall. Where did they get the book and what were they looking at? Was it just a coincidence or were they getting closer to making a connection? This little group would now be getting more attention that was for sure!

CHAPTER FORTY-THREE

Finishing up his apple pie, Harry sat back in his chair sipping his coffee. "I seem to recall the Pi Kappa Alpha Chapter at the University of Michigan was sanctioned at one time due to a hazing incident. I really don't recall the details, but I think someone died. I remember it had an effect on all the chapters nationwide and for a while we were highly scrutinized but surprisingly national Greek organizations lobby for lenient policies and so many of these hazing incidents are swept under the carpet or discounted as boys being boys."

The group talked about a recent hazing death that was in the news.

"Unfortunately, I don't see anything happening in the near future that would prevent these incidents from happening. The Greek system goes back as far as the 1800s and have the reputation of helping men to develop lifelong friendships as well as being a staple of the American college experience."

"Well, I'm just so happy that nothing happened to you," Gertie said patting him on the leg.

"Actually, it was a great experience," Harry agreed. "I was happy to be part of it. Some of my closest friends were my fraternity brothers."

"They're going to toss us out of here," Thelma noted as they were the last table occupied and the staff were clearing up around them.

Harry looked at his watch. "I'm going to have to take off mom.

I have an early conference call in the morning that I want to prepare for. Thanks for the invite. It's always a pleasure to see everyone."

"I'll walk out with you Harry," said Lucy gathering up her purse. "Thanks Aunt Alice, I really enjoyed dinner."

As they prepared to leave, Kelly came up to Lucy and said, "Were you serious about having lunch Detective Amos?"

"Of course I was Kelly. When would you like to get together?"

"Maybe sometime in the next week or so? Finals are over in a couple of days, and I'll have some time before graduation."

"Perfect!" Lucy smiled. "I gave you my card. Do you still have it?"

Kelly nodded

"Give me a call and we'll set a date!"

Harry and Lucy took their leave and the ladies said good night to one another and headed back to their apartments.

Alice turned on her heel and headed for the library to do a little research. Harry's comments about fraternity hazing incidents bothered her. Her interest piqued, she settled at the computer and started "googling" fraternity hazing and for the next hour or so read articles and commentaries about the subject. There was one notation about an incident at the U of M but no details were provided. Rubbing her eyes and stretching her back she was surprised to see it was almost 10 p.m. Shutting down the computer she made her way back to her room.

After dinner, Lucy went back to her apartment and got on her computer to do a little research on fraternity hazings. When Harry recalled the sanction on the Pi K A chapter at Carson's alma mater, a light bulb went off in her head. It was well known that Carson James was a practical joker. Could there have been any involvement on his part in that hazing fatality? It was a long shot but at this point she was ready to grab at any potential connection to this case.

Typing in the words University of Michigan, Pi Kappa Alpha, and hazing on a google search she received a number of hits.

Reading through the articles they verified that a sophomore, Timothy O'Connor had died from alcohol poisoning at a fraternity hazing on September 15, 1989. While there was a suspension of activities at the Pi Kappa Alpha chapter, a case could not be made that there was any foul play on the part of the fraternity and the death was ruled as accidental.

Lucy pulled the yearbook out of her bag and leafed through the book to the Pi K A picture. No Timothy O'Connor. "Of course not," she thought, "if he was rushing, he wouldn't be shown as a current Pike fraternity member." Turning next to the pages for the sophomore class she stopped when she came to the name Timothy O'Connor. Smiling up at her was a picture of a young blonde man. "Bingo," she muttered. Finally, a possible connection. Timothy O'Connor was attending the U of M at the same time as Carson James! Shutting the yearbook and turning off her computer Lucy made a note to contact the University of Michigan in the morning to get more details.

CHAPTER FORTY-FOUR

Lucy and Arnie met up for coffee the next morning after their morning briefing. Lucy told him about her discovery of the fraternity hazing at Carson's time at the University.

""I'm going to make a phone call to the University to see if I can get some more information," she said adding some creamer to her cup.

"Why don't we start by calling Trevor?" suggested Arnie. "He was there too. I'm sure we can get a more personal perspective by talking to him. Less red tape too."

"Great idea! You two seemed to have bonded, you want to make the call?"

"Sure. I'll give him a shout," he said looking in his wallet for Trevor's card. Thumbing through his wallet he found the card.

"Voicemail," he said ending the call.

"Trevor seems pretty good about returning calls," Lucy remarked. "It will be interesting to hear his take. I think I'm going to go ahead and make some calls to the University myself and then we'll compare notes," she said getting up and slinging her purse over her shoulder. "I'll catch up with you later."

Arnie nodded and started going through his wallet. "Might as well clean it out," he said as he saw Lucy looking at the wad of receipts and cards he was holding in his hand.

"I am shocked that you found his card so quickly," she laughed. "What is all that stuff?"

Arnie looked offended. "It is an 'organized mess' as Louise

calls it. Kind of like your desk," he said smugly.

Lucy simply nodded and headed out of the coffee shop.

Since the coffee shop was next to the station so it didn't take her long to get settled back at her desk and start looking at the notes she had made last night from the articles she had found on the internet. She had noted some names of the Director of Student University Involvement and the University President and thought that would be a good place to start.

As she expected, Lucy was transferred from Department to Department before she was finally able to get the extension of the President's secretary.

"Provost's office Marilyn speaking." A voice answered.

Lucy sighed. "I am trying to reach the office of President Moore," she said with exasperation. "This is Detective Lucy Amos with the Elmwood Police Department in Ohio. Can you PLEASE connect me?"

"Sure thing Detective, please hold," she said and soft music filtered through the receiver.

"How's it going?" asked Arnie as he sat down at the desk next to hers.

"I think it would have been easier getting a hold of POTUS," she snarled. "I swear if I am transferred to one more..." speaking back into the phone she said, "Yes, I am trying to reach President Moore's office," and looked at Arnie waiting for another transfer.

"Oh!" she exclaimed in surprise as the person on the other end announced herself as his secretary.

"This is Detective Lucy Amos with the Elmwood Police Department in Ohio. Before we go any further, may I please have your direct extension? I think I have spoken to every department in the University trying to reach you. Uh, huh," she said as she jotted down a number, "perfect! Thanks."

Lucy explained the purpose of her call and his secretary explained that President Moore was tied up for the morning, but she would be sure to have him return the call at his earliest convenience in the afternoon.

Hanging up Lucy sat back in her chair.

"Tell me you have heard from Trevor! It actually may be faster to drive to Michigan at this point!"

"Well, I got my wallet cleaned out, maybe you could use the time while you're waiting to do the same with your desk," he said looking pointedly at the stacks of papers in front of her.

"Touché'" she countered. "I wish they would call back. I hate this waiting around!"

At that moment their cell phones rang simultaneously.

Arnie hummed the song from the Twilight Zone and walked back to his desk answering his phone, while Lucy did the same.

"Detective Amos this is Wayne Moore with the University of Michigan returning your call. I'm in between meetings so thought I would take a chance to catch you."

"Thank you, President Moore. I appreciate your prompt response."

"My secretary tells me you were asking about the hazing incident with the Pike's a number of years ago."

"That is correct sir. I was able to find some of the information on the internet, but I was wondering if the University held any other records that we may be able to look at."

"Offhand I can't tell you for sure, but I can have Helen do a little research. I suppose I should make this easy and take care of this rather than waiting for a subpoena?"

"That would certainly help expedite the process," Lucy agreed. "I think the information may be important to an investigation we have going on here in Ohio."

"Anything you can share with me?" he queried.

"Not at this moment, but once I have an opportunity to look at any records you may have it may be necessary to talk to you again. At that point, I'll probably be able to give you more information."

"Fair enough," he said. "I will have Helen get right on this. Is this the best number for her to reach you?"

Lucy confirmed the number with him. "Let's give her a couple of days to track this down. I will make this her priority."

"Thank you, President Moore. I appreciate the help."

"We'll be in touch Detective. Have a pleasant day."

Lucy looked over at Arnie who was jotted down notes while cradling his cell phone between his ear and shoulder. She gently tapped him on the shoulder and mouthed "Put him on speaker."

Arnie nodded. "Say Trevor, Lucy is available now, would you mind if I go ahead and put you on speaker?"

"Go ahead," Arnie said.

"Hi Detective Amos. As I was telling your partner, I'm a little uncomfortable talking about this over the phone. It's been awhile since I've thought about that night but as you can imagine, it's not something I could easily forget."

Perched on the edge of Arnie's desk Lucy asked, "How close are you to the University?"

"About a 45 minute drive, why?"

Looking at Arnie Lucy said, "Perhaps we can arrange to meet you in Michigan. We may be paying a visit to the University so we can meet you somewhere close by."

Arnie looked at Lucy questioningly.

"Sure, that would work," he said hesitantly. "What are you doing at the University if I may ask?"

"Just doing a little field work. Let me clear it with our supervisor and we'll get back to you with a day. Would that work?"

"Sure, I'll wait for your call," he said and hung up.

"Ever been to Michigan?" she asked Arnie as she picked up the phone to call Lieutenant Sharpe.

CHAPTER FORTY-FIVE

Alice sat at her kitchen table reviewing her "timeline". She added "Pi Kappa Alpha" and put a question mark after it. Was there a connection between the killer and Carson James being part of a fraternity so many years ago? It didn't seem likely, but it certainly was something to consider. And did Kelly really see a copy of the yearbook that they were looking at the night before? If she did, where did she see it? She added "U of M yearbook" to her list as well.

She headed back to the library to do a little more "research." When she got there someone else was using the computer, so she decided to take a seat and wait for them to finish. She picked up a newspaper and looked for the crossword puzzle and found that someone had already started it. Alice looked at the answers they had written and shook her head. She began muttering to herself as she wrote over their answers and entered her own. Engrossed in her efforts she barely noticed when the person using the computer got up and started walking out of the room. Looking up she saw it had been Judge Lambert. "Don't bother saying hello or anything," she thought as she put down the newspaper and headed for the computer.

"Alice, we've been looking all over for you," Faye said entering the library. "We missed you at breakfast and were worried. The shuttle will be here in a little while. Do you need anything from the grocery store?"

"I could use a few things. I have a list in my apartment."

"Go get it and I'll be happy to pick them up for you," said Faye cheerfully.

"No," said Alice. "I think I'll go with you."

Later that afternoon, the foursome sat in Alice's apartment.

"Are you going to movie night this evening?" Thelma asked as she dunked a donut into her coffee.

"What's playing?" asked Gertie grimacing watching Thelma take a bite of the soggy donut.

Alice got up and looked at the calendar on her refrigerator. "Beetlejuice."

Faye clapped her hands. "I love that movie. I'm definitely going."

Alice sighed, "Sure, I'll be there too."

"What's the matter Alice?" Gertie asked.

"I honestly don't know," she said. "I just keep thinking about Carson James. I know it's crazy, but I feel like there's something more I should be doing to help Lucy find the killer."

"If Lucy and her team can't solve it, what do you possibly think you can do?" Thelma asked. "It's time to let it go Alice. Let Lucy do her job. She'll figure it out."

"I suppose, but I feel like I'm getting closer to putting some pieces together. I know you all think I'm crazy, but I'm going to figure this thing out – you just watch!" she said with determination. "I'll make some popcorn for the movies tonight," she said changing the subject.

"I'll make up a pitcher of margaritas," Gertie volunteered.

"Sounds like fun," said Faye. "We all could use a little levity." Reaching out her arms for someone to pull her off Alice's couch, she said, "Remind me to sit at the table next time!" Thelma laughed and helped her to her feet.

While Alice and her friends planned their evening, Lucy and Arnie started white boarding their own information on the case to date.

On the board they had listed Carson James in the center of the board outlining the circumstances of his death, his time at University of Michigan, the fraternity, and his time at the University of Illinois. Radiating from this information, arrows pointed at numerous possibilities including Jackie, Robin, Chef Lewis as well as Trevor.

"Jackie had motive based on her relationship with him. She claims their breakup was her idea, but she could have been dumped by him." Arnie noted.

"Robin sounds like she may have also had designs on Carson," said Lucy making a note under her name. "Could she have been angry enough to do him in?"

"That brings us to Trevor. We need to take a deeper look at the details of the will. I know he wasn't anywhere in the proximity when Carson was poisoned but if he was in a position to receive a lot of money, he certainly could have had someone help. I'm thinking this is a little farfetched but let's not rule him out yet."

Lucy agreed. "This looks pretty weak," she said as she eyed their notes. "Now that Lieutenant Sharp has given us the go ahead, hopefully we can get something from the University and by talking to Trevor again. I went ahead and made reservations at the Marriott. I figured we could leave after lunch tomorrow and drive straight through. You ok with that?"

"Sure," Arnie said putting on his jacket. "Louise and I have dinner plans with the kids tonight so I'm going to head out. See you in the morning."

Lucy waved absently at Arnie as she turned back to the white board. She made a few more notes, put down the marker and realized she hadn't made plans for Quigley while she was in Michigan. She pulled out her cell and made a few phone calls but had no luck finding anyone to watch him. As she started to call a local boarding facility her phone chimed. "Amos," she answered.

"How's my favorite gumshoe?" asked Harry.

"Oh my God," Lucy laughed. "Gumshoe? Where did you come up with that?"

"I have been exploring all of the synonyms for "Detective" in my Thesaurus. "Private eye, snoop, PI, sleuth, dick," he said with mock seriousness.

"Harry, you have way too much time on your hands."

"Pretty much," he agreed. "So, what's cookin' good lookin'?"

Grinning, she started packing up to go home. "Arnie and I

have to make a trip to Michigan for the Carson James case, and I just realized I need to make arrangements for Quigley while I'm gone. I was just getting ready to call Paws on the Lake to set up boarding.

"How long will you be gone?"

"We should just be a night or two at the most. Missing me all ready?" she teased.

"Actually, I was thinking that maybe I could watch Quigley for you, but of course you'll be missed as well." He added quickly.

"That is really sweet of you Harry, but I couldn't impose."

"No imposition at all. The little guy is kind of growing on me and it will give us a chance to bond." He joked.

"Are you sure? That would be wonderful."

"Absolutely. Do you want me to come get him, or do you want to drop him off? That way you can see my condo and I might even have dinner ready for you when you get here…."

"Harry, you are my hero," sighed Lucy as she switched off the lights and headed out the door. "Let me pack up his things and I'll bring him over. What's a good time?"

"Give me a couple of hours. Do you like salmon?"

"Yum! I'll pick up a bottle of wine. See you soon."

CHAPTER FORTY-SIX

Lucy pulled into Harry's driveway at 7:00. Attaching Quigley's leash to his collar, she sat him down on the driveway and grabbed a bag with his treats, food, bowls, and some toys.

Sniffing his way towards the front door, the little dog marked his territory along the way, then satisfied, allowed Lucy to make it to the doorbell.

Harry opened the door wearing a chef's apron and a dishtowel slung over his shoulder. He gave Lucy a quick kiss and bent down to pet Quigley.

"Oh, my goodness, it smells delicious in here!" Lucy said taking in the aromas coming from the kitchen.

"Thank you ma'am," Harry said bowing. "Welcome to my home," he said gesturing around him.

"It's wonderful Harry! You've got a great eye for decorating."

Harry laughed. "I'd love to take the credit but of course my mother took control, but I must admit she did a great job."

Taking the wine from Lucy, Harry headed towards the kitchen. "So, Quigley, looks like you and me will be hanging out together," he said looking over his shoulder. Reaching into a bag he had on his granite countertop he pulled out a large bone, bent down and gave it to the dog.

Quigley grabbed the bone and trotted over to a corner and began gnawing on it.

Lucy laughed, "That thing is almost as big as he is. That will keep him busy while I'm gone. Thanks Harry. You are so sweet."

Harry handed Lucy a goblet of wine. "I'm actually looking forward to it. It gets a little lonely here sometimes. It will be nice to have some company. Hungry?" he asked turning to the oven.

"Famished," she said taking a seat at his kitchen island. Looking around the house she noticed some artwork hanging on various walls. Getting up from the kitchen stool she went to exam each painting. "These are beautiful! Did you get these while you were travelling?"

"Look a little closer at the signature," he said pulling a dish out of the oven.

Lucy bent closer to a painting of a beach and read 'G. Smith'. "Your MOM painted these?" she gasped.

"She sure did," he said proudly.

"Unbelievable! These are amazing. What talent!"

Walking over to stand next to her, Harry looked at the painting she was observing. "Mom met dad while she was majoring in Art. They married before she graduated but she continued to paint throughout their marriage. She sold quite a few of them. Dad was so proud of her."

"I can imagine. Does she still paint?"

"No," he said heading back to the kitchen. "Once dad passed away, she seemed to lose interest. That's why I'm so glad she is at the Manor. Meeting your aunt and the other ladies has put some of the spark back into her. Come on over, dinner is served," he said motioning towards a seat at the table.

Chatting over dinner, the couple laughed over some of Lucy's stories from past cases and the antics of her co-workers in the squad room and Harry shared stories of his travels, so the time passed quickly.

Lucy pulled back from the table and rubbed her stomach. "I am so full I don't know if I can move. Harry, that was delicious. You put my cooking to shame."

Quigley sat quietly looking up at Lucy.

"I bet you have to go outside," she said. Taking his leash from a hook where Harry had hung it, she bent over to attach it to his collar. Laughing she said, "Any more of those meals Mr. Smith and I'm going to need to buy some larger jeans."

Harry took the leash from Lucy's hand. "How about if I walk Quigley and you do kitchen duty?"

"Absolutely!" she agreed and started cleaning off the table.

While Harry and Quigley were outside, Lucy finished up the dishes, poured herself another glass of wine and sat on Harry's over-stuffed sofa, listening to the music quietly playing in the background. Taking in the surroundings she felt a sense of peace and belonging. "This is nice," she thought, laid her head back on the couch cushion and closed her eyes.

Sometime later Lucy awoke and was startled to see that the room was dark and an afghan had been draped over her. Pulling off her shoes, she laid down on the couch, pulling the afghan up to her chin and immediately fell asleep again with a smile on her face.

CHAPTER FORTY-SEVEN

Opening her eyes, Lucy smelled coffee brewing and sun streaming through the sliding doors to the backyard. "Oh my gosh," she sat up abruptly, "what time is it?" she thought as she looked at her watch and saw that it was seven o'clock. The sliding doors opened, and Quigley and Harry entered the room from outside. Quigley scrambled over to Lucy and jumped up on her lap, licking her face.

Harry hung up the leash on the hook, went to the coffee pot, poured a cup for Lucy, handed it to her and sat next to her on the couch. "Good morning," he said casually.

Lucy ran her hand through her hair and groaned. "I am so embarrassed," she moaned.

"I don't know what happened. I was so relaxed after your marvelous dinner I sort of fell asleep," she finished lamely. "I am so sorry. Why didn't you wake me?"

Harry smiled and ran his hand across her cheek. "You looked so cute laying there, I couldn't bring myself to wake you up. Quigley and I tucked you in and went into my room, watched the news, and then hit the sack ourselves. And – no apologies needed," he added "Even though this wasn't how I pictured our first night spent together," he said tongue in cheek.

Lucy blushed. "I am the worst dinner guest ever. And now I have to get out of here or I am going to miss report. I haven't even packed for my trip yet."

Pulling on her shoes, she said, "Harry, I can't thank you

enough."

She stood up, rubbing Quigley's head then hugged Harry. "Are you sure you're ok watching my little guy?"

"Are you kidding? We're already best friends, right Quig-man?"

"His dog food is in the bag I brought over, and he gets a treat after his walk. He'll be fine while you're gone for the day, but don't let him alone more than 8 hours or you may come home to a surprise."

"Lucy, we'll be fine. Just have a safe trip and I hope it yields some good information for your case."

Walking her to the door, he leaned down and kissed her on the lips. "Call me and let me know you got there safely."

"I will," she said and kissed him again before walking to her car.

Quigley and Harry stood at the door and waved to her as she pulled out of the driveway.

Lucy made it to her house in under twenty minutes, threw some clothes in an overnight bag, noticed her answering machine blinking but made a decision to check it later, locked her door, and got to the station just as report was beginning.

Plopping down in a chair next to Arnie, he leaned over and whispered, "Late night Detective Amos?" as she elbowed him in the ribs.

Lieutenant Sharpe went over the days' roster and updated bulletins then turned to Lucy and Arnie.

"So, you two are heading for Michigan today?" he queried. "What's your agenda?"

Arnie brought everyone up to date on the case and looked at Lucy.

"Our plan is to get a better picture of Carson James while he was a student at U of M and look at his student records to see if we are missing any piece of the puzzle. We are also going to be re- interviewing his best friend who happens to be the executor of his estate. We believe that something may have transpired while he was either in under-graduate or graduate school which may have led to his murder. We know it's a stretch but at this point we're kind of at a dead end with the case."

"Keep me up to date," Sharpe said as he closed his notebook. "That's it everyone. Be safe out there today." As the rest of the staff headed out the door, Sharpe turned to Lucy and Amos. "I'm counting on you two to come up with something. The Mayor is breathing down my neck on this one."

"I understand Lieutenant," Lucy said. "We definitely need a break and we're hoping we'll find it in Michigan."

Putting a tootsie roll pop in his mouth, he paused a moment and said, "I know you two are doing the best you can. There's no doubt in my mind if anyone can solve this sucker it will be you guys." Patting Arnie on the back, he walked towards his office.

"What say we plan on being on the road in an hour," said Arnie.

"Sounds like a plan. I'm going to finish up a few emails. I'll meet you by the car."

CHAPTER FORTY-EIGHT

Movie night was set up outside on the grounds of the Manor. Ken had installed the outdoor movie screen and the residents were spread out either on lounge chairs, blankets or wheelchairs as Chef Lewis's staff worked overtime in serving small hors d'oueves, finger sandwiches and healthy fruit cups. The four-some chose to sit on a blanket and pulled out the popcorn and margaritas they had prepared for the evening.

"Isn't this fun?" Faye asked as she took a long sip from her glass.

"I have to admit," Alice said, "it is nice to get outside and have a little fun."

Kelly walked over to the ladies with a tray of sandwiches. Looking at the popcorn and margaritas she laughed. "How about a couple of sandwiches and fruit?" she asked bending down to let them pick.

Kelly's hair was pulled up in a ponytail and she wore a red checkered shirt and cutoff jeans.

Reaching for a sandwich, Gertie commented " You look very cute tonight Kelly."

"Thanks Mrs. Smith. Chef Lewis gave us permission to stay and watch the movie after we were done serving the guests. I invited Adam to come. He should be here soon. I'd love to have you meet him!"

"We would love to!" they all agreed. "You know where to find us," said Thelma as she laid back with her hands behind her head.

The movie began shortly afterwards, and the residents watched intently for the next hour and a half, some laughing uproariously at Beetlejuice's antics. When the show was over, Ken switched on the outside floodlights, and everyone began gathering up their blankets and lawn chairs while those that needed assistance were wheeled back to their rooms by an aide.

As the ladies were folding up their blankets, Kelly and Adam walked over. Kelly made the introductions.

"How did you enjoy the movie?" asked Faye.

"It was cute," said Adam as he swatted at a fly that was buzzing around Kelly's head. "I've never seen it before. We sat with my Aunt Audrey. She didn't seem too impressed."

The ladies looked at each other as if to say, "what a surprise," but Gertie said, "Well it doesn't appeal to everyone's taste but it was a nice night out."

"We're going back to her room to visit with her a little longer," said Kelly as she grabbed Adam's hand.

"It was very nice to meet you all," he said politely. "Kelly really loves you guys!"

"Well thank you Adam," Alice smiled. "She really seems to like you as well!"

Blushing, Kelly pulled Adam toward the Manor. "I'll see you all this weekend!" she said waving over her shoulder.

"What a cute couple," sighed Faye. "Makes me feel like I'm one hundred years old."

"Well, we're certainly closer to a hundred than we are to 18," remarked Alice as Faye swatted her with her now empty canvas bag.

Walking back to the Manor, Gertie said, "Alice, I almost lost it when I saw your expression when Adam said his Aunt didn't seem to like the movie."

"That old bag probably hasn't smiled in years. Her face would probably crack." Alice said.

"Can you imagine having to be in front of her when she was a Judge?" shivered Faye. "She probably gave everyone a life's sentence."

The foursome gave each other hugs and headed back to their apartments agreeing to meet up for breakfast at 8:30 a.m.

Alice put on her nightgown and robe, brewed herself a cup of tea and sat down to watch the evening news. As she was beginning to doze there was a light tap on her door. Getting up to answer it, she looked in the peephole to see Kelly standing there.

"Kelly is everything ok?" she asked.

"I'm sorry to bother you Ms. Campana," Kelly said. "I just said goodnight to Adam and was going to head home but wanted to tell you that I remember where I saw the yearbook like you had the other night. It is in Judge Lambert's apartment. Isn't that a coincidence? I wanted to tell you before I forgot. Sorry to bother you."

"No bother at all dear," said Alice. "Would you like to come in for a cup of tea?"

"No, thanks very much. I better get home, or my parents will start to worry. Good night and see you this weekend."

Looking at the clock, Alice decided it was still early enough to call Lucy. After a few rings Lucy's answering machine picked up. Alice waited for the beep. "Lucy, I found out where Kelly saw the yearbook. Give me a call!"

CHAPTER FORTY-NINE

Lucy and Arnie were on their way to Michigan by 11:30. They stopped two hours into the trip and had lunch at Perkins. Lucy pulled her notebook from her purse as she sipped on her iced tea waiting for the food to be served.

"I was able to talk to President Moore's secretary, Helen, before we left, and she said to stop by her office when we get in and she'll help us any way she can. They're located in the Fleming Administration building.

"Sounds good," said Arnie as the waitress set a plate of pancakes and sausage in front of him.

Lucy looked at her chef salad and then back at Arnie's dish and sighed. "That sure looks better than mine."

Arnie poured blueberry syrup over the pile. "Two days with Louise not looking over my shoulder. I'm going to make the best of it." He flagged the waitress to the table. "Could I have some whipped cream please?"

Lucy laughed. "I hope I can get you home before you have "the big one." I don't want that on my conscience." Shrugging, she poured Italian dressing over her salad while looking enviably at his plate.

"Harry is watching Quigley for me while I'm gone," she said casually.

Arnie raised his eyebrows. "You mean you haven't kicked him to the curb yet? Oh wait, you'll do it after he watches the dog, right?"

Lucy kicked him under the table. "Why is it so hard for you to believe that I may actually be in a relationship?"

Arnie snorted and wiped some whipped cream from his mouth. "How long have we been partners?"

"A little over three years…"

"Correct! And during the three-year period, how many schmucks have you dated?"

Lucy paused and counted on her fingers. "Well, there was the fire fighter," she began.

Arnie held up one finger and said, "How many times did you go out with him?"

"We went out for a couple of months."

"What happened to, Joe, wasn't it?"

"Yes, it was Joe and I ended it because he was too vain."

Arnie held up a 2nd finger, "next?

"That would be Bob, who owned his own construction company."

Arnie laughed. "That's right, 'Bob the Builder.'"

Lucy smiled. "I forgot about that. You really got a kick out of saying that – over and over and over…"

"And what did Bobby boy do to earn his walking papers?"

Lucy sighed, "He smacked his lips every time he took a bite of food. It drove me nuts!"

Arnie held up a third finger and waited for her reply.

"All right, I get it! I am a little picky."

"Ha," Arnie snorted. "We would all place bets on how long it would be before you would dump them."

"What? That's horrible!" she stammered. Taking a sip of her iced tea she asked "how much was in the pot and who won? Tell me you aren't betting on poor Harry!"

Tactfully changing the subject, Arnie said. "I wonder if the Secretary was able to find any documentation on the hazing incident."

"I hope so. My gut tells me that somehow Carson James was involved in it. Now whether that has to something to do with his death is another story."

Finishing their meals, Arnie motioned to the waitress for the check. "Man, I am stuffed. You may have to drive since I'm in a sugar coma."

Lucy began to dig in her purse for her wallet.

"I'll get this one," he said. "You can get dinner."

"Fine," she said zipping up her purse. "So, do you guys have a bet going on Harry or not?"

"Yep." he said as they walked out of the restaurant. "A couple of the guys are already out. They thought Harry would be history by now."

Unlocking the car door, Lucy glared at Arnie over the roof of the car.

"You guys are unbelievable."

"I've gotta admit Amos," Harry said as he got into the car and buckled his seatbelt. "This is one for the records. Maybe he's "the one." Wouldn't that be something?"

Lucy rolled her eyes. "I'm glad I could provide you all with a little entertainment. We have about another hour or so before we get there, so take a nap!"

"Not going to argue you with you there." He said as he laid the seat back and closed his eyes.

Lucy put the car into gear and headed back on to 75 north towards Ann Arbor.

CHAPTER FIFTY

Alice woke up early the next morning and no matter how hard she tried, could not fall asleep again. Giving up, she threw off her covers, put on her robe and trudged to the kitchen to make a cup of tea. She found her timeline and next to yearbook added Audrey Lambert's name next to it. As the microwave beeped, she reached into the cupboard to get a teabag and gasped. That was it! That was the missing piece! When she had seen Robin rush out of Carson James' office, she had seen Judge Lambert sitting nearby watching and smiling. She had found it peculiar but with all the commotion, had put it out of her mind.

Putting the teabag in her hot water, she sat down at her kitchen table to think a moment.

What could that mean? Did it mean anything at all? Maybe she was smiling about something altogether different. No, she was pretty sure that Judge Audrey Lambert was almost waiting for something to happen.

"Alice you are grabbing at straws," she muttered to herself. Looking at the clock, she sighed. It was only 6 a.m. and breakfast didn't start until 8. Turning on the television, she sat in her recliner and started watching the news on Channel 3. The "deal guy" was demonstrating some luggage, jumping on it, throwing it on the ground and even crawling into it. The anchors laughed at his antics, talked about what a great deal it was, then switched over to the weather. It looked like it was going to be another beautiful week. She closed her eyes for a moment and when she opened them it was almost 7:30.

She made her way to the bathroom, threw some water on her face, ran a comb through her hair, brushed her teeth and went in to change.

Forty-five minutes later she was sitting at breakfast with her friends. She decided not to mention the yearbook to the others yet. They would probably scold her again about how she needed to stop worrying about the case.

"Harry called this morning and said he is watching Quigley for Lucy." Gertrude said. "She and her partner are heading to Michigan today to work on a case."

"I called her last night, but she didn't pick up," said Alice. Are you sure they are leaving today and not yesterday? It's not like her not to call me back."

"No," answered Gertie. "He specifically said they were leaving today but he had Quigley since last night so she could get on the road by noon. Maybe she went to bed early."

Alice shrugged. "She'll call me when she gets back."

Faye spread some jam on her toast. "It sounds like this might be getting serious. Harry and Lucy that is."

"You all are such romantics," grumbled Alice. "It's only been a couple of months. Give it some time and she'll find something wrong with him."

"Excuse me?" said Gertie raising her eyebrows.

"I only mean that Lucy always seems to find a way to end a relationship when she thinks they are getting too serious. I don't mean there is anything wrong with Harry! But trust me, she'll find something!"

"Maybe Harry will find something wrong with HER," Gertie said defensively.

Thelma placed her hands on each one of their arms. "Let's not go there again. Harry and Lucy are both adults and we need to let nature take its course."

Alice looked at Gertie. "I'm sorry Gertie. Harry is a lovely man, and any woman would be lucky to have him."

Gertie smiled at Alice. "And Lucy is a doll. Let's keep our fingers crossed that it works out. I think they make an adorable couple."

"By the way," Thelma asked. "Has your sister met Harry yet?"

"No," Alice said. "My sister and her new husband are always travelling somewhere. I get so frustrated with her. She needs to give her daughter more attention. She's always been self-centered."

"Well thank goodness Lucy has you," soothed Faye.

Alice smiled. "She and I have always been close. She's the daughter I never had."

The foursome took their beverages and went to sit outside on the back patio. They sat quietly listening to the birds chirping in the background.

"Lucy said she has a friend who has a house on Kellys Island," Alice said. "She thought maybe the two of us could get away for a long weekend this summer."

"How nice," Faye smiled. "What is Kellys Island and where is it?"

"Are you serious Faye?" asked Alice. "You don't know where Kellys Island is?"

Gertie looked at Alice and said, "I'm afraid I've never heard of it either."

Alice looked at Thelma. "Tell me YOU know where Kellys is?"

Thelma looked at Gertie and Faye. "Ohio has a number of cute little islands to visit west of here close to Cedar Point and Catawba. If you've never been to Kellys or Put-in-Bay, you're missing a real treat. They have golf carts or bicycles to get around the island. Lots of cute shops, restaurants, historical monuments and bars – lots of bars!" she laughed.

"It sounds delightful!" Faye said. "That's something I definitely need to go see."

"Me too!" said Gertie. "I might even take my paints and easel with me. It's been a long time since I've been anywhere that's inspired me. It sounds like just the right place."

"I'll talk to Lucy to see how many the house can accommodate."

"No," said Gertie. "We wouldn't interfere on your time together. Maybe we could find something for the three of us."

"We'll see," said Alice. "It would be a lot of fun with all of you there as well."

"Maybe Harry would want to go too," suggested Gertie.

The group cheerfully talked about getting some more information on housing availability and looking at the ferry schedule.

The time passed quickly and by the time they made their way back into the Manor, some of the residents were heading to the dining hall for lunch.

"Oh my gosh," said Faye. "I feel like all we do is eat and sit. We have got to start walking or something. I've put on 5 extra pounds over the winter."

"That's a great idea Faye," said Gertie. "Let's start walking together after breakfast. I know we have our recreational therapist work with us, but now that the weather is nice again, let's plan on getting out of here more."

"I'm not sure if I've even got any good walking shoes," said Alice. "I'll have to check my closet, but it sounds like a plan. Anyone up for some lunch?"

"What the heck," said Faye. "What's another couple of pounds?"

Alice went back to her apartment after having a salad and some soup for lunch. She wanted to see if she had any shoes that would be appropriate for walking and thought she might take a short nap.

Getting ready to put her key in the lock, she noticed the door wasn't shut tightly.

Alarmed, she slowly pushed the door open and peeked inside to see if anyone was inside. She cautiously looked through each room and satisfied no one was there shut the door firmly behind her. "I have to be more careful about locking up when I leave," she thought and headed to look in her bedroom closet. She found a pair of old tennis shoes, dusted them off, slipped them on and happily they still fit. She turned on the TV in her bedroom, pulled back the covers and lay down. She immediately fell asleep and as she dozed, Carson James' killer walked by her apartment door. Noticing the door was now firmly shut, they smiled and wondered if nosy Alice Campana had a little scare when she saw her door wasn't locked when she got back to her room.   They had been very careful not to disrupt anything in the apartment when they broke in.   It was a little surprising to see a piece of paper on her kitchen table with notes about Carson James' murder, but nothing that gave any cause for alarm... at least for now. However, the woman was tenacious enough to warrant keeping an eye on her.

CHAPTER FIFTY-ONE

As Alice took her afternoon nap, Lucy and Arnie had arrived at the campus of University of Michigan. The campus was quiet since many of the students had gone home for the summer, but there were still quite a few young men and women either walking or bicycling around. Lucy pulled into a parking lot, locked up the car and they headed towards the Administration building following the directions that the lot attendant had given them.

"Boy does this bring back memories," Lucy smiled. "College was the best time of my life!"

"I didn't go away to college," said Arnie. "I went to the local community college for a while and then decided that I wanted to be a cop like my old man."

They came to an area that looked to be the center of campus where students were throwing Frisbees, sitting around on blankets or sunbathing, enjoying the early summer weather.

"This must be the Diagonal," said Arnie. "The kid at the parking lot told us we'd be walking through it so we must be headed in the right direction."

"There is supposed to be a brass block "M" somewhere around here," said Lucy. Stopping to ask a couple walking by they pointed to where it was located. Lucy said to Arnie "Let's take a minute and check it out."

Arnie agreed and they found the symbol a few minutes later. As they stared at it, a young co-ed who was in the vicinity came up to them and asked if they would take a picture of her next to the inlaid "M."

Lucy took her phone and snapped a couple of pictures for her.

"Thanks so much," the girl said looking at the pictures that

Lucy had taken. "I've been wanting to get a picture for a while. My dad used to kid me about the "curse", so I've been keeping my distance until my first exam was out of the way."

Lucy and Arnie looked at her questioningly. "Legend has it that if you step on the "M" before you have taken your first blue book exam you will flunk your exam." She laughed. "Back when my dad was here, he said that in order to reverse the curse students would run naked from the bell tower, it's now called Burton Memorial Tower, to the cat statues by the National Science Museum and back to the bell tower at midnight before the bells stopped chiming. Thanks again!" she said and jogged off towards a cluster of buildings.

Arnie shook his head. "I hope they got to at least wear a pair of shoes," he said. "Wow, what a sight that must have been!"

Lucy laughed. "We probably should head over to the Admin Building."

Entering the building, they asked someone for directions to the President's office. They took the elevator to the 2nd floor and soon found the office. A woman sat at the reception desk tapping at her keyboard and looked up as they entered the room. "You must be the Detectives from Ohio," she said standing up to shake their hands. "I'm Helen Winston. We spoke on the phone."

Lucy and Arnie both shook her hand. "Thanks for letting us come by on such short notice."

"No problem at all," she smiled and went back to her desk. "President Moore sends his apologies that he couldn't be here to meet you, but he has been tied up attending budgetary meetings."

Arnie nodded. "We understand. Like Detective Amos told you, we really don't want to create any extra work for either of you. Hopefully you were able to find the information on the hazing incident?"

Helen turned around and opened a door to her credenza. She pulled out a folder and handed it to Arnie. "It was actually easier than I anticipated," she said. "I've reserved the small conference room down the hall for the two of you to work. Let me show you where it is."

Following her down the hallway, she unlocked the door to a mid-sized room where a conference table that could easily seat 12 people, a white board, some markers, and a tray with bottled waters were ready for them.

"Would you like me to call catering to have them bring you up some sandwiches?" she asked as she wiped at some non-existent dust on the table.

"Oh, my goodness no!" Lucy exclaimed. "You have done more than enough. We can't thank you enough for your hospitality!"

"If you could just show me where the restrooms are?" Arnie asked.

"Of course," she said and headed out of the room with Arnie behind her. Turning around to address Lucy she said, "If there is anything else you need, please just dial extension 101 she said pointing at a phone on the table."

"I'm sure we'll be just fine, but thanks again. We'll bring the files back to your office when we're done."

"Perfect! Follow me Detective!"

While Arnie took his "bio break," Lucy opened the folder and pulled out its contents. There were numerous newspaper articles, legal documents, and papers with handwritten notes.

Lucy sorted the paperwork into piles trying to organize them into categories.

Arnie re-entered the room, took off his suit jacket and rolled up his sleeves. Looking around the room he said, "That was nice of them to give us a workspace. Looks like we have everything we need." He opened a bottle of water and offered it to Lucy.

"Thanks," she said absently taking the bottle while continuing to concentrate on a newspaper article she was reading. Looking up she said, "I separated the paperwork into different piles. I thought it might be quicker to start with the newspaper clippings."

"Ok," Arnie said. "I'll tackle the handwritten notes and we can leave the legal stuff for last."

Reading out loud Lucy began "Timothy O'Connor, 19, died September 15, 1989, at University Hospital. Cause of death has not been released."

Pulling another article from the folder, "Timothy O'Connor, a sophomore at the University of Michigan died shortly after arriving at the University of Michigan hospital. Cause of death appears to have been alcohol poisoning. Witnesses state that Mr. O'Connor was participating in a hazing activity at the Pi Kappa Alpha fraternity. Local law enforcement is investigating his death as suspicious."

Lucy stood up, took a marker from the table, and started writing on the white board. She wrote "Timothy O'Connor" and September 15, 1989.

Arnie was reading some handwritten notes. "It says here he was from Mt. Pleasant, Michigan."

Lucy noted that on the board.

"He graduated from Sacred Heart Academy High School, was an honors student and on the cross country, basketball and track teams."

Again, Lucy listed it on the board.

"He sounds like he was a kid any parent would be proud of."

The two spent the next three hours looking through the folder and entering information both on the white board and in Lucy's notebook.

Engrossed in their work, they were startled when there was a tap on the door and Helen Winston stepped into the room.

"I'm going to be heading out for the evening. Is there anything I can get the two of you before I leave?" she asked.

Arnie looked at his watch. "I can't believe it's after 5 already. No thanks again. I think the two of us will head to the hotel and check in for the evening. Do you mind if we take this file with us, or would you prefer for us to leave it here?"

"Of course, you are welcome to take it with you," she assured them. "Where are you staying?"

"The Marriott down the street," said Lucy as she started packing up her briefcase.

"Would you like me to recommend some restaurants in the area for you?"

"That would be really nice," smiled Lucy. "Thank you."

"May I have a piece of paper?" asked Helen. "I'll jot down some of the local sports bars that have decent food and some of the chain restaurants. Do you prefer anything in particular?"

"Just as long as they have cold beers," laughed Arnie. "We aren't picky about the food."

"Speak for yourself! The food has got to be good too. I would die for a big, juicy steak about right now."

Helen wrote down some names and drew a makeshift map to show them where they were located in conjunction to their hotel. "I'll be back at my desk around 8 a.m. I've reserved this room for you again for tomorrow. I hope you both have a pleasant evening."

Arnie and Lucy thanked her again and she closed the door behind her. They could hear her high heels clicking down the hallway.

"That is one efficient broad," said Arnie.

Lucy looked at the list of restaurants and pointed at a name and said, "Let's try this one after we check in. She noted they have great burgers. Yum."

"Sounds good to me," Arnie said. "You suppose we can leave our notes on the board?"

"We'll lock the door behind us," Lucy replied. "I don't think anyone will bother it."

They made their way back to the car, taking their time to look at the buildings, enjoying the scenery and saying hello to young passers-by.

They checked into their hotel, spent some time unpacking and freshening up then met back in the lobby an hour later.

Lucy threw the car keys to Arnie. "Do you mind driving? I'm bushed!"

Arnie caught the keys. "Yeah, I'm kind of tired myself. Let's grab a burger and call it a night. Bed is gonna feel pretty good tonight."

They each ordered a cheeseburger, fries and a beer and listened to country music playing

in the background.

"I'm thinking maybe another couple hours going over the file should do it and then we can catch up with Trevor. I told him we'd probably meet up with him mid-afternoon and he was ok with that," said Lucy as she poured more ketchup on her fries.

"I feel like we got a pretty good background on what transpired with the hazing," Arnie said after he took a sip of his beer. "We know that Carson was in the fraternity at the same time, but I just feel like we're swinging for the fences with a pretty small bat."

Lucy laughed, "Huh?"

"We just don't have a lot of good information yet to get this thing solved."

"I know. I was hoping we'd find the answer staring us in the face. Maybe Trevor will help us put it altogether."

After paying for their meal, the couple made it back to the hotel, said goodnight and agreed to meet in the lobby at 8 a.m.

After Lucy washed up and put on her nightgown, she plugged in her cell phone to charge it and gave Harry a call.

"Hope I'm not calling too late," she said when Harry finally answered.

"No not at all! Studley and I just got back from a walk."

"Who is Studley?" Lucy asked.

"You know. AKA Quigley, Quig-man and now Studley!"

"Oh my gosh!" Lucy chortled. "Where did you come up with that one?"

"Seriously Lucy. Where did you come up with the name Quigley for God sake? I'm surprised he doesn't squat when he pees. How emasculating! So I decided to call him Studley. Much more macho."

"Wow! I'm glad I'm coming back tomorrow. You'll probably buy him a spiked collar and a leather leash next."

"Now there's an idea," Harry laughed. "So, how's it going?

You guys are coming back tomorrow already?"

"On one hand I'm glad that you two are getting along, on the other I'm feeling like I should postpone my homecoming. Are you dating me just for my dog?" she laughed.

"Detective Amos, I do believe you are jealous. Let me assure you we are both missing you! Have you solved the case?"

"I wish! It's like looking for the proverbial needle in a haystack."

"Well, Studley and I have the utmost faith in you. Give me a call when you're about an hour from home and I will have dinner ready and waiting for you!"

"Harry, you do not need to go to any trouble. You have done more than enough by watching Quigley for me. How about if I take you out somewhere?"

"Sounds like a plan but it really has been no trouble at all. I enjoy having the little guy around. I might just have to go buy myself a dog. They are great companions, and he is a captive audience. I got home from work and told him all about my day!"

Lucy laughed. "Well, I'm glad the two of you are bonding. I'm going to crawl into bed. I'll give you a call when I'm about an hour away tomorrow. Have a nice evening and give my boy a hug!"

She thought about giving her Aunt Alice a call but decided that she may be asleep by now. She would catch up with her when she got home.

CHAPTER FIFTY-TWO

When Alice awoke from her nap, she was surprised to see that it was almost 5:00. Deciding to forgo supper she gave Gertie a call to let her know that she wouldn't be coming.

"Are you feeling all right Alice?" asked Gertie with concern.

"Fit as a fiddle! I'm really not hungry so why stuff more food in my pie hole?"

Gertie laughed. "Well, you could come join us for a cup of coffee...."

"No, I'll see you all at breakfast in the morning. I have leftovers in the fridge if I get hungry. It feels good to just relax."

"Ok then. We'll see you around 8," Gertie replied and hung up.

Alice went into her kitchen to fix herself a cup of tea. While the microwave hummed, she glanced over at her kitchen table. Well, that was curious. Her notes were spread across the table, but she was sure when she had left the papers were stacked neatly in a pile. Alarm bells went off in her brain as she recalled the unlocked door when she came back from lunch. Had someone been in her apartment?

The microwave dinged and she jumped at the sound. She walked to her door and made sure the chain was on the door. She shivered. Who could have been in her apartment? Housekeeping wasn't due until tomorrow.

She fixed her tea and sat down at the table, staring at her notes again. The only link to the case was that yearbook. Somehow Judge Lambert was possibly a key. Why would she have a copy of the same UM yearbook that Carson James had? Shoot! She wished she had asked Lucy if she could have kept the copy to study it.

Wait a minute. Maybe she could look on the internet and see if she could find a copy there. She checked her hair in the hallway mirror, slipped on her shoes and locking the door firmly behind her, headed for the library.

Passing by the dining hall, she noticed her friends chatting amiably among each other. She smiled. She was so lucky to have found such great companions!

Finding the library computer unoccupied she got to work and started googling U of M yearbooks. She found hits on the "Micheganensian", its history, how to order one for your student and numerous other articles that she clicked on but was unable to find an actual copy.

She sat back in her chair and thought a moment. She knew where one could be found right here in the Manor but how would she go about getting it? She dismissed the thought of doing another breaking and entering. She smiled as she remembered Gertie's cat burglar garb. Maybe she could ask Kelly to "borrow" it. No, she didn't want to get poor Kelly mixed up in anything. She sighed. Could she possibly ask the Judge if she could borrow it? That brought up another dilemma. How was she supposed to know that the Judge had a copy without ratting on Kelly?

Alice shut down the computer and returned to her apartment. She put on her nightgown and robe and sat down at her kitchen table to review her notes once again and contemplate. She decided the best route would be to ask Lucy if she could look at her copy of the yearbook. It probably was a dumb idea anyway.

She sat back in her chair and started thinking about when Carson James arrived at the Manor. Dunahie had been "transferred" to Corporate, but everyone knew that it was because of his drinking. Carson had been well received by the residents and staff, especially the single ones. She remembered all the whispers in the dining hall from the female residents about what a "hunk" he was and sighs of their lost youth.

It was about the same time shortly afterward that Judge Lambert became a resident. She remembered that because every month the Manor would have a small reception welcoming their newest occupants. The Director would always give a little speech but during this particular reception, Carson James was not present. Chalking it up to being new to the Manor, Jackie filled in for him at the last minute. It was a little awkward, but she did a pretty good job coming up with a welcoming speech. She had the new residents take a little time to introduce themselves and since there were only two – Judge Lambert and Paul Limburgh – they pretty much had the floor to themselves. Paul rattled on about his life- starting from puberty- as far as Alice could remember and by the time it came to Judge Lambert, she stiffly introduced herself as a retired judge from Michigan and the mother of one son. She had sat down quickly as though everyone had heard all they needed to know. Alice recalled looking at her friends as if to say, "Well isn't she warm and fuzzy." From that moment on, everyone pretty much kept their distance from the Judge.

Alice sat upright. Wait a minute – the mother of one son? As long as the Judge had been at the Manor, she had never seen her with a visitor – including a son!

She went into her room, got dressed again and headed back to the computer.

As luck would have it, someone was now using it. "Rats!" she muttered to herself and contemplated having a seat and waiting for them to finish. She walked by, glancing at the screen, and noticed that they were involved in some sort of game. This could take a while!

She decided to wait and took a seat on an overstuffed chair. She picked up a magazine and leafed through its pages glancing up occasionally to see if they were done. Thirty minutes later, there was no sign that they were going to be finished any time soon.

Putting the magazine down, she walked over to the computer desk and stood behind the female resident.

"Well hello Fran," Alice smiled. "I was wondering if you were planning on being much longer? I have some rather important business that I must attend to and would like to use the computer for some research. I really hate to bother you, but I have to have it done by tomorrow morning? Would you be a dear and let me take a turn?"

Fran Cook sighed and said, "Well if you must. I'm so close to beating this level..."

"Thank you so much!" Alice said as she slid the keyboard towards her and clicked on the escape button.

Fran frowned and got up from the chair. "You're welcome," she said a little sarcastically and headed towards the hall. Meeting a friend coming towards her, Fran said in a voice meant to be heard, "Some people around here need to be taught some manners." But Alice was already tapping away at the keyboard, oblivious to her remark.

Entering key words, Michigan, Judge Lambert, family she began searching for anything she could find on Audrey Lambert.

The search returned some articles on Judge Audrey Lambert, Court of Common Pleas in Isabella County. There were numerous newspaper articles outlining her campaign. Under marital status it noted: divorced, one child. There was no other information or names.

She read an interview from what appeared to be a local newspaper regarding her campaign. "Why are you running for public office?" "What would you like to accomplish if elected?" were some of the questions in the article.

All of the replies were standard politician replies about wanting to make the community a safe place, giving back to the community, blah, blah, blah. Again, she mentioned having a son, but no other details such as name or age. Another dead end!

As Alice continued to Google Judge Lambert, she finally found an interview in a newspaper where the Judge mentioned her son, Timothy. Alice jotted down the name "Timothy Lambert" in her notebook. Finally – something to go on.

She then began googling the name "Timothy Lambert" and found numerous hits but nothing that seemed to be connected to Judge Audrey Lambert. "I give up," she sighed.

Shutting down the computer, she stood up, stretched and headed back to her apartment.

CHAPTER FIFTY-THREE

Arnie and Lucy met in the hotel lobby, had a quick bite at the free breakfast buffet and headed back to U of M.

"I made a call to Trevor. He has invited us to meet at his home around 1:00. It's about 45 minutes from here, then we can head back home." Said Arnie. "I went through the file before bed last night and made a few other notes that we can talk about when we get back to the office."

"Thanks Arnie," smiled Lucy as she took a last sip of her coffee. "I can't believe how exhausted I was. I was asleep before my head hit the pillow."

"Ready to roll?" he asked. "I'll drive."

"OK," she agreed. "I'll take us to Trevor's apartment."

When they arrived at the President's office, they were surprised to see President Moore sitting at his desk. Helen stood up from her desk when they entered the room and motioned towards the open door. "I'm glad you are here. President Moore has about 15 minutes before he has to leave and wanted to meet you both." She escorted the two into a spacious office where the President stood up from his desk and came around to shake their hands. He motioned for them to take a seat. Heading back to his chair he also took a seat, adjusted the cuffs of his shirt, and smiled pleasantly at them.

"I hope Helen was able to accommodate you. I apologize for not being here to greet you yesterday."

Arnie smiled back. "Thank you. She took very good care of us.

You've got a great assistant."

Lucy asked, "President Moore, how long have you been with the University?"

"I've been here a little over 10 years now."

"So, you weren't here when the Pi Kappa Alpha hazing incident occurred?"

"No that was before my tenure began. I do believe it was around 1989. I was just finishing up my Doctorate at Vassar. After your call Detective Amos, I did a little research myself. Ugly situation." He said shaking his head.

"We would certainly appreciate any information you can share with us," said Lucy sitting forward in her chair.

"Do you mind if I take a few notes?" asked Arnie reaching in his coat pocket.

"Of course," President Moore said. He pulled out a sheaf of paper from his top drawer and started reading from his own notes.

"The incident began at a rush party at the Pike house. It appears there about 200 students there and a lot of booze was flowing. Some of the new pledges were responsible for organizing the party, Timothy O'Connor, being one of them. The President of the Fraternity at that time was Trevor Rathbun, Vice President was Carson James , Treasurer was Jim Franklin and Fraternity Marshall was Rick Elbert. It appears that Mr. O'Connor died from alcohol poisoning. The parents filed suit claiming the fraternity was responsible for his death but after an in depth investigation the end result was sanctions."

"So, Carson James was here at the same time." Said Arnie as he jotted down the names and information that President Moore was sharing.

"The Vice President of the house is responsible for assisting the President and organizing activities so both Carson and Trevor's name were mentioned in the suit. Both graduated the following Spring around the time the sanction was lifted. May I ask what this is about?"

"We are investigating the death of Carson James and believe

this incident may have some bearing on the case." Arnie said.

"I am sorry to hear that." The President said looking surprised. "That was years ago. It's hard to believe this would be a contributing factor."

Lucy nodded, "We agree, but at this point we are pursuing all possible leads as you can imagine."

He shook his head, looked at his watch and stood up. "I'm sorry but I do have another commitment in about 5 minutes. I wish I were able to spend more time with you. If you need anything further, Helen is at your disposal. Please let us know what transpires if you would please."

The twosome stood up and shook President Moore's hand. "Thank you, sir," said Lucy. "We have everything we need at this point. We appreciate everything you and Helen have done. We'll be in touch if we need anything further."

They walked out of the office with the President and stayed to say good-bye to Helen and give her back her file.

"Those are your copies," she said. "Please feel free to take them with you. I hope they were of some help."

"Absolutely," said Lucy. "You have been a great help. Thank you once again for everything."

Saying their good-byes, they headed back to their car.

"Well, the plot thickens," said Arnie.

"Looks like we'll have a lot to talk about with Mr. Rathbun." Lucy looked at her watch. "We should be about right on time."

When they arrived at his residence, after numerous attempts at knocking and ringing the doorbell no one was there.

"Lovely," muttered Lucy. "I thought you said you confirmed with him that we were coming."

"I did," Arnie said. "Let's give it a little time. Maybe he's running late."

Ten minutes later, a red corvette, top down, rolled into the driveway. Travis Rathbun got out of the car before checking his hair in the rearview mirror.

"Detectives," he said cheerfully. "I am sorry to have kept you waiting. I got caught up in a case. Come on in," he motioned as he unlocked the door and stepped aside for them to enter the house.

If Carson James' condo was a showcase, it was nothing compared to the lavish décor of Travis James' home. Expensive looking oriental carpets were placed throughout the room over hardwood floors. An ebony baby grand piano sat in the corner overlooking an immaculately groomed lawn. The furniture was done in navy and yellow and the whole effect was welcoming. Over the fireplace Lucy noticed the piece of art from Carson James' condo.

Travis walked to his bar and opened a beer. "May I offer you a beverage," he asked. "Beer, soda, bottled water?"

"Water would be great," said Arnie. Lucy agreed and they took a seat on an overstuffed sofa.

Travis sat down in leather recliner, popped up the footrest and sighed after taking a swig of his beer. "Oh man, nothing like a cold one after a day at the zoo. So, tell me, how's the case going?"

"Mr. Rathbun," Lucy started speaking.

"Please, I thought I told you to call me Trevor."

"Trevor," she began again. "We'd like to talk about the night that Timothy O'Connor died."

Putting down his beer, Trevor lowered the footrest on his recliner, stood up and walked over to the fireplace. Placing his hand on the mantle, he turned and faced the detectives. "That was a long time ago," he said running his other hand through his hair. "But it also feels like yesterday – like it's a bad dream you just can't shake."

He sat back down on the recliner, leaned forward with his elbows on his knees and clasping his hands.

"Are you thinking this may have something to do with Carson's death?"

"We're not sure," answered Arnie "but we think it's a possibility."

"Who? How?" he asked.

"Let's start from the beginning," Lucy said softly. "If you could just tell us about the events that led to his death."

"Phew," Trevor whistled. "I'll do the best I can. Carson and I had been elected officers of the fraternity for our senior year. Tim was a pledge and was getting ready to be initiated so we gave him the task of helping Carson to organize our first rush party of the season. It was the usual- lots of booze, invites to new freshmen, the hot sorority chicks and a bunch of our little sisters."

"Little sisters?" asked Arnie.

"Girls on campus who didn't want to pledge to a sorority but wanted a part of the Greek life would be invited to be a "Little Sister". They'd be hostesses for our parties, come to the house and mingle with the brothers and be part of our family."

"Any way, the night of the party everyone was having a good time, we had a couple of freshmen on the line to pledge and Tim was working hard to make sure everything was going smoothly. Carson started teasing him about needing to relax and just to enjoy himself and started giving him mixed drinks – making sure he was actually drinking them. Some of the brothers got in on the act and started pouring Tim glasses of beer and encouraging him to drink yelling "Chug, chug, chug, chug." Tim wasn't a big guy, and it didn't take long for the drinks to have an effect and he started wobbling around the room. Carson took it a little too far and made him start doing jumping jacks, trying to walk in a straight line and telling him he wasn't drunk enough, every good Pike knows how to hold their liquor. So, after a few more drinks, Tim collapsed to the floor, Carson carried him to the couch we all had a few good laughs and the party continued. It was probably a couple of hours later that someone noticed that Tim wasn't moving. We tried to wake him up, but he wasn't breathing. We called 911, the paramedics came and after trying to resuscitate him pronounced him dead at the scene. Man, what a nightmare. The cops came and took everyone's statements before they could leave. The University became involved and pronounced that the house was on notice that an investigation would be held. In the meantime, no more parties, no more new members and Carson and my terms as officers were suspended until further notice. Tim's parents pressed charges against both the house and against Carson and me – citing "depraved indifference" since we were officers. It didn't help that Tim's mom was a Judge herself. We thought for sure we'd be doing time. However, the court made a ruling that it was involuntary man slaughter, and the penalty would be sanctions on the house for the remainder of the year. We had to do community service for 3 months. I guess they figured that having to live with the consequences of our actions was a penalty in itself. I think the Chapter had a lot to do with helping Carson and me avoid jail time. The whole situation is one of the reasons I went on to Law School."

"You said Tim's mom was a Judge," asked Lucy, alarm bells going off in her head.

"Yes," said Trevor. "She had a different last name than Tim. It took a while before we realized it was his mom."

"Judge Audrey Lambert?" Lucy asked tentatively.

"Yes, that's it!" he said. "If looks could kill. She kept staring at us throughout the trial. She was pissed when the verdict was read. I think she wanted us locked up for life. I can't blame her. It has to be a bitch losing a child. I wonder what happened to her?"

"We've got to go," she said looking at Arnie.

"What?" Arnie asked looking confused.

"We've got to go NOW!" Lucy repeated, standing up and heading towards the door.

"Thanks for your time, Trevor," Arnie said looking over his shoulder as he followed Lucy out the door.

CHAPTER FIFTY-FOUR

Elmwood Manor was hosting its third annual Senior Fair. Representatives from health insurance carriers, local clinics offering free blood pressure checks, TTY telephone representatives, fitness demonstrations and other senior facing vendors were setting up their tables for a three-hour event.

"I hate these things," mumbled Thelma. "It makes me feel old."

"I love all the 'freebies,'" said Faye. "It's a great way to stock up on hand sanitizers, jar openers, back scratchers and great bags to use at Kroger's."

"It's all junk," said Alice. "Everyone loves it because it's free and then it ends up in the trash!"

"Not me!" Faye replied. "I have a bag full of stuff that I use. If you don't want it, I'll take it. The grandkids use some of it in their backpacks for school and camp."

"They're having a cooking demonstration this year," said Gertie. "I know they're trying to sell their skillets, but I love taste testing."

"I see Judge Lambert is going to be a guest speaker. She's talking about Identity Theft and Seniors." Thelma noted as she looked at the program.

"Is she?" asked Alice curiously. "What time is she scheduled to speak?"

"Looks like from 1 until 2," said Thelma.

"Hmmm," said Alice formulating a plan.

"Is that a good 'Hmmm' or bad 'Hmmmm...'" asked Faye.

"Just 'Hmmm," said Alice. Changing the subject, she looked over Thelma's shoulder at the program. "She'll be speaking right after lunch. Hope we can all stay awake!"

At 11:00 the event was open for business and the foursome spent an hour visiting different tables with Faye stocking up on the free giveaways. As they entered the dining room to sit down for the lunch, Faye straggled behind them toting three full bags.

Thelma started laughing as she watched her shove them under the table. "You look like a bag lady!"

"Laugh all you want," Faye said defensively. "Just remember the next time you are struggling to open a jar that you could have snagged one of these," she said pulling a round rubber circle out of her bag before she sat down.

"Ladies and Gentlemen," William Dunahie spoke into the microphone. "Thank you all for attending our Third Annual Senior Fair. We have certainly come a long way since I first introduced the idea three years ago. Thank you to all our vendors for being here and to University Hospital for sponsoring our luncheon. Let's give them a round of applause." After polite clapping from the residents, he continued. "One of our own residents, the esteemed Judge Audrey Lambert will be speaking directly after lunch about identity theft and the senior population which I'm sure you will all find enlightening. We are looking forward to it, Judge," he said looking at Audrey Lambert.

She nodded stiffly in his direction and attempted to give a weak smile.

"Everyone please enjoy your lunch," he said and sat down at a table with what appeared to be representatives from Corporate headquarters.

"Notice how he mentioned how he started this event?" asked Alice. "Looks like someone is trying to impress the brass."

"It appears that Mr. Dunahie has proven himself. I suppose he'll be reinstated as Director again," Gertie sighed.

The ladies enjoyed lunch which consisted of baked chicken, green beans, mashed potatoes, a side salad, and a slice of cake for dessert.

"I could go for a big slice of pepperoni pizza," said Faye. "I am so tired of chicken."

"Hey, I have a great idea," said Gertie perking up. "How about we walk over to that new Italian restaurant that opened up down the street. We keep saying we are going to start walking. It's a beautiful day."

The ladies agreed to meet in the lobby around 5:00.

As the dishes were being cleared away, Mr. Dunahie rose again and introduced Judge Lambert.

Alice rose from her seat and said softly to Faye, "I'm going to run up to my apartment. That lunch isn't sitting very well if you know what I mean. I'll see you at 5:00."

Faye whispered back, "I hope you feel better. Let me know if you need anything!"

"I'll be fine. Just a little indigestion!" and she walked out of the room.

As she headed down the hallway, she could hear Audrey Lambert's voice coming from the microphone introducing herself. Pushing the elevator button, she waited impatiently for it to make its way to the first floor. When the door opened, she quickly entered, jabbed the button for the 2nd floor and hit the arrows to close the door. When she got off, she smiled with relief as she saw the housekeeping cart sitting outside of one of the resident's rooms. Peeking her head in the room she saw Maria wiping down the resident's kitchen counter humming along to music that she was listening to with her earbuds. Startled, Maria looked up and said, "Ms. Campana you scared me!"

"I'm sorry Maria. You have a beautiful voice by the way."

Maria smiled. "I love to listen to music when I work. It makes the time go by so quickly and it gives me more energy! How can I help you? Is your room not cleaned to your liking?"

"No, it looks perfect as usual," she lied. "I'm wondering if you could possibly let me in to Audrey Lambert's apartment. She is giving a speech and asked if I could grab a sweater for her. They keep those rooms so darned cold!"

"Of course, Ms. Campana," Maria smiled as she dug in her pocket for her Master Key. "Let me open the door for you."

"No, don't bother," Alice smiled reaching for the keys. "I'll let myself in and bring these right back!"

"Well, I suppose that would be ok," Maria said.

"Of course, it is. That way I won't get you off schedule!"

Maria smiled and handed her the keys. "It's the one with the pink band on top. You are such a nice lady, Ms. Campana!"

Alice smiled back at her and took the keys. "I'll be right back!"

Hurrying down the hallway, Alice came to Audrey Lambert's apartment and with hands shaking unlocked her door. Quickly scanning the apartment, she saw a bookshelf next to her TV She made her way across the room and started looking through the books to see if she could see the yearbook. Where was the darn thing? She moved into the bedroom and again quickly scanned the room without seeing it. She didn't have much time as she was only supposed to be there to get a sweater. She looked in the closet. Just like hers, the top shelf was inaccessible without a chair. Drat! She took a sweater from the closet and went back into the living room. Grabbing a pen, she let herself out of the apartment using the pen to keep the door from shutting tight.

Making her way back to Maria who was again humming to some tunes, she waved her hands in the air to get her attention, pointed to the sweater, and mouthed "thank you" and placed the keys on the table. Maria smiled back and went back to her dusting.

Alice then hurried back to the Judge's apartment, looked over her shoulder to be sure no one was around and let herself back in, shutting the door quietly behind her. Looking at her watch she noticed she still had about 35 minutes before Judge Lambert's talk was scheduled to conclude. That should give her plenty of time.

Alice went back into the bedroom and rehung the sweater, went to the kitchen and dragged one of the dining room chairs into the bedroom to look at the top closet for the book. Finding a shoe box, she opened it and saw pictures of the Judge with a handsome man and young boy and various other pictures of the young man at different stages of his life. Putting the lid back on she wondered what had become of the young man and why she never saw him visit his mother. She carefully looked through the bedroom nightstands, being careful not to disturb its contents. She then went into the bathroom, opening the vanity doors and drawers and a magazine rack attached to the vanity. "Someone likes to read while they do their business," she thought.

She pulled the chair back to the dining room table and started searching the living room again. She went through the bookshelves one more time with no luck. Sitting down on the couch, she looked down. There it was! Sitting atop a pile of old newspapers she recognized the cover from the yearbook that Lucy had shown them. On the end table she noticed a framed photo of the young man. He was dressed in a graduation gown with the Judge, and she supposed her husband on either side of him. He was holding his diploma and grinning. The Judge was looking at him proudly and she could see a younger version of the woman. She appeared softer and was actually quite attractive. Next to the picture was a small vase. An urn? A small, framed newspaper clipping sat next to it. Reading the heading "Timothy Cooper September 15, 1989" she proceeded to read the obituary. Alice gasped! That poor woman had lost her son! Looking through the yearbook, she found Timothy Cooper's picture. He was there the same time that Carson James was there. There had to be a connection! Alice carefully set the picture back on the end table and was putting the yearbook back on the pile of newspapers when she looked up to see Judge Audrey Lambert!

CHAPTER FIFTY-FIVE

Grabbing her cell phone from her purse, Lucy dialed her aunt's phone number. When her answering machine picked up, she hung up. She then dialed her remote access to her own home answering machine and listened to the message that her aunt had left a few nights before when she was asleep on Harry's couch. "Lucy, I found out where Kelly saw the yearbook. Give me a call!"

"Oh no," she moaned.

Arnie opened the passenger door and got in the car looking at Lucy. "Do you want to tell me what's going on?"

"Shut the door, I'll tell you on the way." Lucy explained as she threw the car into reverse and squealed out of the driveway.

"Judge Audrey Lambert is a resident at Elmwood Manor. My Aunt, your mom and their buddies have been snooping around trying to find out who killed Carson James and I'm afraid they may be getting a little too close for their own good!"

"Whoa," Arnie said, "Timothy Cooper's mom is living at the same Retirement Home where Carson James was Director. Tell me that isn't a coincidence."

"Of course, it isn't," Lucy snapped. "My guess is she had this all planned out and was keeping him under her radar. We have to find out when Judge Lambert became a resident. I'll bet it was shortly after Carson James showed up."

Arnie pulled out his cell phone. "Call Elmwood Manor, Elmwood, OH," he spoke into the phone. "Call Elmwood Manor Detroit Road, Elmwood, Oh?" was queried back. "Yes," he said.

"Calling Elmwood Manor, if you would like a text sent please press #."

"Elmwood Manor, Robin speaking, how may I help you?"

"Robin, this is Detective Arnie Fischer, can you look something up for me please?"

"Of course, Detective Fischer."

"Can you please tell me when Carson James became Director and also when one of your residents, Audrey Lambert moved into the Manor?"

"Sure thing, hang on one moment please."

Arnie sat impatiently listening to the music playing in the background when Robin clicked back on the phone. "Carson started his new position on August 5th of 2015 and Judge Lambert moved in mid-September of that same year. Is there anything else Detective?"

"No, Robin, thanks very much!"

Arnie turned to Lucy. "She showed up around a month after he came on board."

"That's no coincidence," Lucy said stepping on the accelerator. "Why isn't my aunt answering?"

"It's the middle of the day," Arnie said. "I'm sure she's somewhere with her friends. Slow down, you're going to either going to get us killed or picked up by the local highway patrol."

"Ok, Ok," Lucy said as she left off on the gas pedal. "I'm just being paranoid. We should be there in about 4 hours. I'll call her again in a little bit."

"Let's think this through," said Arnie as he pulled out his notebook. "Judge Lambert's son dies at the same Fraternity where Carson James is V.P and all he gets is a slap on the hand, in her eyes. That's a long time to hold a grudge though. Why wouldn't she have done something sooner?"

"I don't know," said Lucy rubbing the back of her neck while clutching the steering wheel with her other hand.

"Why don't you let me drive?" asked Arnie. "You look beat."

"I'm fine," said Lucy. "I need to drive. I'd go crazy if I had to just sit there."

Arnie got back on the phone. "Julia, this is Detective Fischer.

Can you do me a favor and do a little research on Judge Audrey Lambert? Anything you can dig up on her in let's say the last 30 years would be great. OK Julia. Thanks."

Julia Davis worked with the Elmwood Police Department and was responsible for doing research when needed.

"Let's see if we can find out what Audrey Lambert has been doing these last 28 years. If anyone can find anything, our tenacious Julia will."

Lucy nodded and looked at her watch again then concentrated on the road ahead of her.

The two rode in silence for the next 30 minutes. Lucy handed her cell phone to Arnie. Can you please hit redial and call my Aunt Alice?" she asked him. Arnie hit the redial button and waited until Alice's voice mail picked up. "Nothing yet," he said quietly. "Lucy I'm sure she's fine. Why don't you call one of her friends?"

"I don't have any of their numbers but believe me from now on I will."

"Hey, why don't you call Harry and have him give his mom a call?" he suggested.

"Oh my gosh, why didn't I think of that?" she brightened. "His number is in my contacts."

Arnie dialed the number and handed the phone to Lucy.

Harry picked up on the 3rd ring. "Hey good lookin', are you an hour away?"

"Harry," she almost shouted into the phone, "I'm about 3 and a half hours away. I need you to do me a favor and give your mom a call to see if she knows where my Aunt Alice is. Could you do that for me please and call me right back?"

"Of course," he said, "is everything ok?"

"I'll tell you everything soon, but first I have to make sure my aunt is ok."

"Sure Lucy. Hang tight. I'll call you right back!"

Five minutes later Lucy's phone rang.

"Did you find her?" she practically shouted into the phone.

"I talked to my mom. Your aunt was at some kind of senior event at the Manor, had lunch with the ladies and then excused herself afterwards and said she wasn't feeling well. I have Robin checking her apartment. Wait, this is her calling...." He put her on hold and came back on the line a few minutes later. "She isn't in her apartment so that's a good thing. At least we know she isn't ill. Mom said they are all meeting up at 5:00 in the lobby to go grab a pizza. In the meantime, they're looking around for her. I'm sure she'll show up at 5. I'll keep you posted. Ok?"

"Ok," she said. "Thanks Harry, please call me as soon as they find her."

"Of course," he said and hung up.

Arnie's phone rang. "Fischer here," he answered.

"Uh huh, Ok, I see, great idea. Ok, Julia I'll wait for your call."

Lucy looked over at him. "What?"

"It seems like Judge Audrey Lambert dropped off the radar after her son died. Julia's going to try to get in touch with her ex-husband. She'll call us back."

"God," Lucy moaned....

Lucy looked at the dashboard. "Crap, we have to stop for gas."

They drove a little further and they got off on the next exit. Arnie got out and started filling the tank. "I'm going to hit the can. Do you want anything to drink?"

"No, I'm good. Please hurry..."

"I'll do the best I can..."

Lucy laughed. "I'm sorry Arnie. I'm being overly dramatic. Take your time and if you could bring me a diet that would be great."

The hose clicked off, so Lucy got out of the car and put the gas cap back on and heard Arnie's phone ringing inside the car.

She opened the passenger door and grabbed the phone. "This is Detective Amos."

"Oh, Detective Amos, this is Julia Davis. Did I call the wrong number?"

"No Julia, Arnie stepped away for a moment. Were you able to locate Mr. Cooper?"

"As a matter of fact, I was.   Mr. Cooper said his ex-wife had a breakdown after the trial and attempted suicide. Luckily her paralegal found her in her office bathroom, called the paramedics and she made it through. Afterwards they had to have her committed to a psychiatric facility where she stayed for 3 years. She attempted to return to her law practice for the next ten years, but she missed court dates, failed to follow up with her clients and basically had to hang up her shingle. She had a brother who lived off the grid in New York and went to live with him. Mr. Cooper said the brother was what he called "squirrely." After she moved in with him Mr. Cooper said he lost track of her."

"Did you happen did get the name of Judge Lambert's brother? "asked Lucy as Arnie made his way back to the car.

"Mr. Cooper said he heard that the brother passed away about 3 years ago."

"Thanks Julia, this is great info," said Lucy.

Lucy handed Arnie his phone and walked over to the driver's side. She sat down, clicked on her seatbelt, and said, "Judge Lambert is our perp – I'm sure of it now." She proceeded to tell Arnie what Julia had told her.

"It sure sounds like it could be her," Arnie agreed. "But we still need proof."

"If it's her, we'll find it." Lucy said with determination. "But first I have to find my Aunt Alice.   God, I wish Harry would call..."

CHAPTER FIFTY-SIX

Alice opened her eyes and found that she was tied to a chair. Her head ached and she felt slightly nauseous. She closed her eyes quickly hoping to stop the room from spinning. Taking deep breaths, she tried to peek through half open eyes to look around the room. Where was she? She closed her eyes again and tried to remember the last thing that came to her mind.

She remembered having lunch with her friends then excusing herself. She recalled taking the elevator to the second floor and talking with Maria. That was it! She went to Judge Lambert's apartment and the last thing she could remember was seeing the Judge standing over her and then a blinding pain as something crashed over her head.

Taking a few more deep breaths she attempted to open her eyes again and was able to focus a little better. Moving her head slowly she took in her surrounding and saw dresses, coats, and blouses on hangers. She was in a closet! She was in Judge Lambert's closet! How long had she been unconscious? Light filtered in from under the door enabling her to see; at least for now. So, it wasn't night yet unless the light was coming from the bedroom lamp.

Trying to move her hands, which were tied behind her, she found she was unable to do much more than wiggle her fingers. Her ankles were tied together, and a pair of pantyhose was wrapped around her waist binding her to the chair as well. Well, this was a real pickle! What the heck was the old bat thinking? Sure, she shouldn't have been in her apartment, but her reaction was a little extreme. Another wave of nausea washed over her, so she shut her eyes and continued to take deep breaths until it passed. "Think Alice, think," she thought to herself. "What would they do on CSI to get out of this situation?" Her head ached. All she wanted to do was to sleep. Her chin dropped down and once again she fell into a dark abyss.

At 5:00 Gertie and Thelma waited for Alice to join them.

"Where is she?" asked Gertie.

"I'm getting concerned," agreed Thelma said. "No one has seen her since lunch."

Faye joined the pair. "Robin said they looked in her apartment earlier and she wasn't there. Do you think she left the building and went for a walk or something?"

"Let's walk over to the restaurant, maybe she's waiting for us there." Gertie said heading towards the front door.

Just as she was reaching for the door handle, Harry entered the building.

"Harry," she exclaimed. "What are you doing here?"

Planting a kiss on his mother's head, he then held her at arm's length and asked, "Have you seen Alice?"

"No! Harry, I'm scared. We were just about to walk over to the pizza place down the street. We were all going to have dinner there. Maybe she's there waiting for us."

Harry nodded. "Wait here. I'll go check," he said and rushed out the door.

The three friends took a seat on a bench and holding hands waited for Harry to return. Ten minutes later he walked into the building shaking his head. "Not there."

"Oh my," said Thelma putting her hand over her heart. Making the sign of the cross she offered up a silent prayer.

Harry walked over to the reception area. Robin was shutting down her computer and smiled up at Harry. "Well hello Mr. Smith. Are you having dinner with your mom tonight?"

"Robin, do you have a PA system here?"

"Well, yes. Why?"

"Can you possibly make an announcement? Can you page Alice Campana?"

"I don't know," she said cautiously. "We only page people in case of an emergency."

"Consider this an emergency," he said. "No one has seen her for hours."

"Of course," she said and reached over to flip on a switch on a blinking panel.

"May I have your attention please?" her voice carried throughout the building. "Would Alice Campana please report to the front reception desk? Again, would Alice Campana please report to the front reception desk? Thank you!"

Curious residents walked over to the friends asking if there was anything they could do. None of them recalled seeing Alice since the luncheon.

Minutes went by and Alice was not to be found.

"Can we check her apartment again?" Harry asked Robin.

"Of course," she said grabbing her master keys and led the way towards Alice's apartment.

The group looked throughout the apartment without any sign of Alice's whereabouts.

"Maybe we should call the police?" suggested Faye, wringing her hands.

"I've got to give Lucy a call." Harry said reaching for his phone. "I promised her I'd let her know if she didn't show up to meet you at 5."

He walked into the bedroom and made the call. A few minutes later he exited the bedroom and said, "She and Arnie should be here in about 10 minutes. We're going to meet her here. Let's just take a seat and wait for her."

Nodding, the ladies found a seat and quietly waited for Lucy and Arnie to show up.

CHAPTER FIFTY-SEVEN

Alice felt something cool on her forehead and opened her eyes to see Judge Audrey Lambert standing there holding a cold compress.

"Hello Ms. Campana," she said cheerfully. "I thought you were going to sleep the night away."

Alice' mouth was dry. "I'm sorry I've been poor company," she managed to croak.

"Well, you haven't lost your sense of humor I see," smiled the Judge. "I'm going to untie you now, but you have to promise to behave yourself and not make a noise."

Alice nodded and felt the bonds holding her arms behind her being cut. Her arms fell to her sides and prickles of pain streamed through them as her circulation slowly returned. Her ankles were also set free and finally the pantyhose holding her to the chair was removed.

Grabbing her arm and nearly lifting her off the chair the Judge said, "I want you to join me in the kitchen. I've made you some dinner."

Alice almost screamed in pain as she stood up. Her head was spinning, and her legs felt like dead weights. She stumbled but the Judge continued to hold her upright and finally

she made it into the kitchen. A pot of something was simmering on the stove and smelled quite good if she wasn't so nauseous.

Alice looked towards the door and the Judge smiled. "Don't

even think about it," she said and held up a small handgun that was sitting on the counter next to the stove. A bottle of Jack Daniels was next to the gun and a glass that was almost empty.

She helped Alice to a chair and went back to the stove to stir whatever was cooking.

Returning to the table after filling her glass with more alcohol, she sat next to Alice, folded her hands on the table and said, "So you finally figured it out."

Alice sat silently.

"I knew you were trouble the moment I set eyes on you," the Judge continued. "Always sticking your nose into everyones' business." She laughed. "I had my own little nickname for you – Alice CamPAINa."

"Clever," smiled Alice weakly.

"You are quite the little sleuth," she continued. "I would watch you on the computer and after you left would look at the computer's history to find out where you had been searching. You were very interested in me. I'm flattered. You also seemed to want to know about the University of Michigan and the Pikes. Oh yes, Ms. "Campaina," I was keeping my eye on you!"

Alice continued to keep her silence, waiting for Audrey Lambert to continue her tirade.

Becoming more agitated, Audrey Lambert walked back to the stove, stirred the pot, pulled a glass out of the cupboard, and filled it with tap water. She brought the glass over to Alice and pushed it in front of her.

Alice gratefully took the glass and took a long swallow feeling the cool liquid run down the back of her throat. She almost whimpered in relief.

The Judge walked over to the end table, picked up the photo of her son and brought it back to the table where Alice sat quietly.

She sat down, staring at the picture. "My sweet Timmy," she said. She turned the photo towards Alice. "Wasn't he handsome?" She took another sip from her glass.

Alice looked at the picture. "Keep her talking," she thought to herself. "Maybe she'll pass out from all the alcohol she's drinking."

"Yes," said Alice. "He was very handsome. Can you tell me about him?"

She turned the picture towards herself again and started speaking. "His name was Timothy Alan O'Connor, the joy of my life. I couldn't have asked for a more perfect son. From the day he was born he never gave me a moment's trouble." She stared intently at the picture and swallowed the last of the liquid in the glass. "He had just graduated from high school in this picture. He would be entering the U of M in the Fall. He wanted to go into law like his mother. I had him work in my office doing some paralegal work during the summer and he seemed to thrive on all the detail and minutiae. I knew he would make an amazing lawyer."

She got up and refilled her glass. Holding the bottle up she asked Alice, "would you like some?"

"No thank you," Alice said, "but I would love some more water."

She refilled Alice's glass and came back to the table with her own glass filled to the brim.

"He had a great freshman year, had a 4.0 average and worked at my law firm for another summer. He wanted to be a Pike. He was going to get initiated that Fall, his sophomore year. His father was a Pike when he went to U of M." She stopped talking as if she had lost her train of thought. She banged her glass down on the table and Alice jumped.

"Those sons of bitches killed my boy! That damn Carson James killed my boy! My life was over. I swore to God that he would pay, him and Trevor Rathbun," she said mimicking the name. "Snooty bastard. He would have been next but I'm just so tired..."

Draining her glass, she stood up. "Enough talk. You and I are going to have dinner together. Our own little 'last supper.'" She laughed at her own joke.

Alice's blood ran cold. "Oh?" she managed to say. "What's on the menu?"

"Mushroom soup. It's to die for!" she laughed again.

"Well, that sounds lovely, but really I'm not hungry."

The Judge turned and looked at her. "You won't have to eat a lot. I learned from my mistake with Carson. I didn't use enough. It took him way too long to die. I waited outside his office every day until I saw Jackie Drake come running out. I knew it was finally over! Took the little bastard long enough."

"Did you make him mushroom soup also?" Alice dared to ask.

"No, I waited until Chef Lewis made his famous Swiss steak and added my own personal supply to Carson's dinner."

"How did you know he would be eating that evening?" Alice asked curiously.

"I made sure he had a plate sent to his office. I called the kitchen myself and said I was Robin Murphy and Carson would like the chopped sirloin. Actually, it couldn't have worked out any better. I waited by the kitchen and saw that little twit Kelly heading towards his office with the tray. The rest was easy. I watched as she went into his office, waited a few minutes, and made a phone call pretending I was one of the residents who thought they smelled gas. When I saw him heading towards the apartments, I slipped into his office, added my death caps and well, you know what happened next." She laughed harshly. "People are so damn stupid!"

She hiccupped and turned back to the stove. Giving the soup another stir, she reached over and grabbed a couple of bowls and started ladling the soup into them.

"Come to think of it," Alice said, "I would love a glass of what you're drinking."

"Don't think I don't know what you're doing," the Judge smiled. "You're stalling. But that's ok, I'll have one with you. We have all night."

She came back to the table with 2 full glasses. After she handed Alice hers, she raised her own glass as if to make a toast. "To Carson James. We'll meet you in hell!" She took a gulp from her glass and looked at Alice. "Aren't you going to drink yours?

Don't waste good liquor."

Alice took a little sip from her glass. "I'm curious. Where did you get the mushrooms? I'm guessing not at Kroger's," she said trying to lighten mood.

"Very good Ms. Campana," said the Judge raising her glass again. "I spent some time living with my brother in New York. He was the one who taught me how to pick wild mushrooms. He made sure I knew which were edible. The Death Cap definitely is not!

I'm not sure why, but I saved some thinking they may come in handy in the future. Isn't that odd how the Universe works?"

She got up again and came back with two bowls full of broth.

"We're going to eat this and when things quiet down out there," she motioned towards the hallway outside the door, "we're going to take a little ride and watch our final sunset together. Won't that be lovely?"

"Oh, are we calling an Uber?" Alice asked sarcastically.

The Judge laughed. "Really Alice you are quite amusing. I wish I would have taken the time to get to know you better. If you must know my car is parked outside the service entrance. We'll take the freight elevator, so we don't run into anyone. God I'm good," she said taking a last swallow of her Jack Daniels.

Holding up her bowl she held it to her lips and took a long swallow. "Bottoms up! It's actually quite good."

Alice pushed her bowl away. "Thanks, but I'm going to pass."

The Judge got up quickly, knocking her chair over in the process. She weaved over to the counter and picked up the handgun. Walking carefully back to the table, she pointed the gun at Alice and said, "Eat your soup!"

"I'm afraid you'll have to shoot me," Alice replied. "I'm not eating the soup."

"EAT THE SOUP!"

Alice pulled the steaming bowl towards her and taking it cautiously in her hands threw it at the Judge.

The Judge screamed as the hot liquid hit her, dropping her gun in the process.

Alice tried to stand but her legs gave out from under her, and she tumbled to the floor. Crawling towards the gun she attempted to grab it while Audrey Lambert continued to howl in pain. Noticing what Alice was doing, the Judge managed to kick the gun away from Alice's outstretched hand throwing herself on top of Alice.

The two began to scuffle, clawing at each other when the apartment door flew open. Lucy stood there pointing a gun yelling, "Freeze, police!"

The two senior women continued to roll around the floor, batting at each other and throwing punches.

Lucy watched in amazement as her aunt pinned the Judge down in a half Nelson, looked up at Lucy and said, "It's about time!"

Lucy moved into the room with Arnie, Gertie, Faye, Thelma, and Harry right behind her. Arnie rushed over to the women, gently moved Alice off the Judge, pulled the Judge from the floor and walked her over to Lucy. Lucy pulled some handcuffs from her belt and put them on the Judge's wrists.

Alice's friends rushed over to her all talking at once.

"Are you ok?"

"Oh, sweetie you're bleeding!"

"Thank God you're alive!"

"I'm fine," Alice said running her hands over her arms, legs, and face. "At least I think I am. Lucy, the Judge drank some poison mushroom soup. You better call an ambulance."

Lucy got on her radio and called to have a "bus" sent to Elmwood Manor. "You didn't drink any did you Aunt Alice?" she asked breathlessly.

"No dear. I wasn't hungry."

Lucy laughed and gave her aunt a big hug.

CHAPTER FIFTY-EIGHT

Alice sat in her hospital bed surrounded by flowers, balloons, and stuffed animals. Every bone in her body ached and the dizziness, caused from a concussion from the blow to her head, was finally subsiding.

"Well good morning sunshine," said Lucy entering the room with a cup of Starbucks hot tea. "Earl Grey, one sugar, light on the cream," she said handing the cup to her aunt.

Alice gratefully accepted the cup, took a sip and sighed, "Ambrosia! Thank you!"

Lucy sat on the edge of the bed, stroked her aunt's cheek, and asked, "How are you feeling?"

"Like I went a few rounds with Mohammed Ali."

"Well, he certainly would have had his work cut out with those moves of yours!" Lucy laughed. "Remind me never to piss you off."

"Language dear," Alice reprimanded.

"Yep, you're feeling better!"

Alice became serious. "Judge Lambert?" she asked.

"She's going to make a full recovery. The ER doctor was able to reach someone at a hospital in Santa Cruz who has found that administering milk thistle can stop the effects of the poison. I don't know all the details, but it was flown to the hospital here and given to her in time."

"What's going to happen to her? The woman is a few French fries short of a Happy Meal."

Lucy shook her head. "Aunt Alice you are too much! She will be charged with manslaughter, kidnapping and attempted manslaughter but my guess is after a psychological assessment she won't be competent to stand trial. More than likely, she will be confined to a psychiatric facility."

"She killed Carson, Lucy," Alice cried softly. "Someone named Trevor was next in line."

"Once you're feeling better, we'll take your statement. In the meantime, I want you to crawl under those covers and get some rest."

"I don't need to rest, I just want to go home," mumbled Alice but listened to Lucy and slid under the covers. "How did you know where to find me?" she asked as her eyes began to close.

"You told me where to find you," Lucy said stroking her cheek. "When I listened to your message on my answering machine, I knew you wouldn't let it go until you had the yearbook in your hands. When we found out that Carson was at the University the same time that Tim was there, we were pretty sure Judge Lambert was our killer."

"Thanks for saving me Lucy," Alice managed to say and drifted off to sleep.

"You're welcome, Aunt Alice," she whispered and kissed her softly on the cheek.

CHAPTER FIFTY-NINE

When Alice returned home a few days later she was shocked to see a banner hanging over the front door of the Manor.

"Welcome home Alice – Our Hero!"

She made her way carefully through the door, using a cane to keep her balance and was met at the door by her 3 friends. They all hugged her taking care not to hurt her sore body. Lucy held on to her other arm. "Are you sure you don't want a wheelchair," she asked solicitously.

"No, I don't want a darned wheelchair," Alice snapped. "I'm perfectly capable of walking!"

William Dunahie rounded the corner pushing a wheelchair. "Madame, your chariot awaits," he said taking her arm and gently easing her into the chair. "You are our guest of honor. Please allow me to do the honors," and began pushing her towards the dining room.

The room was filled with balloons and banners saying "Welcome home Alice," "Our hero," and "Speedy Recovery." Residents sat at tables and when William Dunahie pushed her chair into the room everyone broke into applause.

Alice's mouth dropped open. "Well for heaven sakes! For once I am speechless."

Everyone laughed. "That won't last long!" someone shouted, and everyone laughed again.

Dunahie wheeled her over to a table and her three friends, Lucy and Harry joined her. Chef Lewis pushed a cart with a cake with lit sparklers over to her, gave her a hug and said with a choked voice "I am so glad you are all right. We're happy to have you home!" and swiped at his eyes to wipe away some tears.

The cake was cut, and Alice spent the next few hours receiving well wishes, cards and small wrapped gifts from the residents.

As the crowd began to disperse, Alice stifled a yawn.

"You must be exhausted," said Faye. "Let's get you back to your room."

"If there is anything you need Ms. Campana, please don't hesitate to ask." said Mr. Dunahie.

"Thank you," Alice said a little taken aback by his attentiveness.

Harry took control of the wheelchair, and the little group made their way back to her apartment.

Lucy helped Alice into her recliner and went into the kitchen to make her a cup of tea.

"We'll let you get some rest," Gertie said. "Call me if you need anything."

"I'm staying with her tonight," Lucy said handing her aunt a cup.

"Oh, Lucy that isn't necessary," Alice said. "The couch opens up into a bed."

Harry laughed. "I'll walk you to your room mom," he said taking Gertie's arm. "It's been a busy day." He gave Lucy a quick kiss on the cheek. "Don't worry about Studley. He's in good hands."

Lucy smiled her thanks and gave him a hug.

Harry, Gertie, Faye and Thelma said their goodnights and left Lucy and Alice alone.

Lucy helped Alice into her nightgown, tucked her in bed and threw a blanket and pillow on the couch. As she began to lay down, she felt like she was being sucked in by quick sand. "Hell no," she said and managed to extricate herself, spread the blanket on the floor and tried to make herself comfortable.

Alice laid in her bed staring at the ceiling. It was good to be home in her own bed, but she couldn't sleep. Without the aid of the medication that she was receiving in the hospital, she began replaying the scenario that had unfolded days before in Judge Lambert's apartment upstairs. She shivered at the thought of a gun being pointed at her direction. What if she threw the soup and it had missed its mark? Would the Judge have shot her? What if the Judge had overtaken her while they wrestled on the floor and Lucy hadn't arrived in time?

She whispered, "Thank you God," as she stared at the ceiling. No more snooping for her – no siree. She continued to toss and turn before sleep finally overtook her.

CHAPTER SIXTY

The next few weeks were a whirlwind with the press calling the Manor asking for interviews with Alice and William Dunahie. They camped outside in the parking lot hoping to catch anyone entering or leaving the facility to get a statement. Some of the residents used this opportunity to grasp their one minute of fame, but were quickly dismissed by reporters when it was determined they were merely seeking attention. Alice did agree to one press conference with Lucy and William Dunahie by her side, but after that stated she just wanted to put the whole episode behind her.

Life returned to normalcy at the Manor, at least for most of the residents. Alice continued to struggle with nightmares and was assured by a counselor, who Lucy insisted that she see, that it was not unusual. She compared it to PTSD that veterans experienced upon their return home. Of course, her three friends were there at her side to help keep her occupied.

The Big Ben puzzle was finally completed, and the foursome had their own little celebration at the pizza house down the street. They toasted their success over a bottle of wine and a pepperoni pizza.

"Lucy made our reservations for Kellys Island," Alice said as she reached for a 2nd piece of pizza. "She was able to find a house that accommodates 12 people. Anyone interested?"

"Interested?" Gertie practically yelled. "You bet I am! Can I bring my paints?"

Alice smiled. "You better! It's about time you dusted off those brushes and easel. You are wasting all that talent."

"Pooh," Gertie dismissed her with a wave of her hand. "It's been so long I'm not even sure if I can do it anymore. How about you two?" she asked Faye and Thelma.

"When are you going?" asked Faye.

"What – you have to check your social calendar?" Gertie joked.

Faye blushed. "No, it's just that I've never been on a boat. I'm a little nervous around water. I never learned how to swim."

Alice patted her hand. "We'll be taking a ferry across the lake. You'll be perfectly safe! We'll be going the 2nd week in August."

"Well, I'm in too," said Thelma. "As long as Lucy doesn't mind us tagging along…"

Alice laughed. "She'll be happy to have you, so she doesn't have to spend all her time entertaining me." She looked at Gertie. "She's also going to ask Harry if he wants to come!"

Gertie clapped her hands in delight. "It will be a party. I can't wait!"

The ladies spent the rest of their lunch talking about their upcoming trip. Since the house came fully furnished with all their bedding, pots and pans, all they would need to bring would be groceries.

"It even has a washer and dryer," Alice remarked. "There is a wraparound porch with a grill and gates, so Lucy is planning on bringing Quigley."

"Well, it sounds wonderful," Faye said. "Thank you for inviting us. I'll definitely think about it."

"There's no thinking about it," Thelma said firmly. "You're coming!"

"We'll see." She said again.

Alice looked over at Thelma and slightly shook her head. "Of course, you can think about it. We have over a month."

Changing the subject Alice said, "Lucy is having lunch today with little Kelly Martin. I guess Kelly is considering going into law enforcement."

"I hope Lucy talks her out of it," Thelma said.

"Why would you say that" Alice said with a puzzled look on

her face.

"It's just such a dangerous profession for a woman. Now don't look at me like that Alice. I know you are very proud of Lucy and all she's accomplished but can you honestly say you don't worry about her?"

"I'm not going to lie," Alice admitted. "Would I rather have her be doing something else? Probably, but Lucy loves what she does, and she does it well. I just try not to think about it."

"Worry is the absence of faith," Thelma quoted.

The waiter came by their table with their checks and a box to bring their leftovers home.

"I'm going to need that walk home," said Faye rubbing her belly.

"Ditto," said Gertie.

The foursome made their way back to the Manor then each headed back to their own apartment with plans to meet up at dinner."

CHAPTER SIXTY-ONE

Lucy made it to the restaurant ten minutes late. Looking around she saw Kelly sitting outside on the patio, sipping on her drink. She brightened when she saw Lucy walking towards her. "Detective Amos," she smiled. "I was hoping you didn't forget."

"Please, call me Lucy. Sorry I'm late. I got caught up with some paperwork and totally lost track of time." She walked over and gave Kelly a quick hug.

The waitress came and took her drink order, handing her a menu.

"I'm just going to have a Cobb salad," Lucy said handing her back the menu.

"I'll do the same," said Kelly.

The waitress took their orders and returned shortly with their iced teas.

"How is your aunt doing?" Kelly asked.

"She's a tough woman," Lucy smiled. "She's going to be just fine. Thanks for asking. How is Adam holding up? It must have been quite a shock for him."

Kelly looked down at her lap. "Adam and I broke up. I think he was really embarrassed. I told him that what his aunt did was no reflection on him, but he said he was going to head back up to New York and stay at his Uncle's place for a while. It's been vacant since he passed away, but Adam still has a key and plans on opening it back up and do a little "introspection" as he said."

She dabbed at a tear coursing down her cheek. "You know, I really liked him a lot."

Lucy reached across the table and took her hand. "I'm sorry. He just needs a little time to process all of this, I'm sure. He'll be back you'll see. Want to make a bet?"

Kelly smiled. "Sure, what are we betting?"

"Loser has to buy the next lunch."

"Deal," said Kelly shaking Lucy's hand.

The two spent the next hour discussing Lucy's job – both the good and the bad. Lucy shared some stories of her past cases while Kelly listened and asking questions occasionally.

"You know it's not all that glamorous," Lucy shared. "It's a lot of overtime and a lot of paperwork. A LOT of paperwork," she repeated.

"It sounds like something I would definitely be interested in," Kelly said. "I can picture myself doing what you do. I'm excited to get started!"

Kelly would be leaving mid-August for college.

"You know, this may or may not be the job for you. It's not unusual to change your mind a number of times until you finally graduate. Either way, let me know if there is anything I can do to help you."

Kelly gave Lucy a hug and the two headed towards the parking lot after Lucy picked up the check over Kelly's objections.

"I only have a few more weeks at the Manor," Kelly said as she opened her car door. "Maybe I'll see you again before then?"

"I'm sure you will! Knowing Aunt Alice, I will probably be having quite a few meals with her and the other ladies. We are taking a little vacation in August and I'm sure I'll have to rein them in on what they are planning on bringing."

Kelly laughed. "Well good luck with that! They are quite a team!"

"You don't know the half of it," Lucy rolled her eyes. "They certainly are a handful. I'm sure it will be a very interesting week."

The two said their good-byes and Lucy watched as Kelly drove off in her little yellow VW Beetle.

She thought back to when she was a college freshman heading off to Bowling Green. She was a little envious of Kelly's upcoming adventures but also glad to have it behind her. She got into her own car and headed back to the office and the pile of paperwork waiting for her on her desk.

When she got to her desk, she found a message that Trevor had called her. Arnie had taken a couple days of vacation. Looking over at her desk she saw a stack of messages waiting for him. Walking over to his desk, she sorted through the messages and saw that Trevor had called him as well.

She sat down her at desk and dialed Trevor's office. His receptionist said he was gone for the afternoon but gave Lucy his cell phone number. Trevor picked up after the 4th ring. "Trevor Rathbun," he said.

"Hey Trevor, Lucy Amos. I see you have been trying to reach Arnie and me. What's going on?"

"Lucy." He sounded relieved. "Thanks so much for calling. I just wanted to find out the status of Audrey Lambert's hearing. I have to say I am a little skittish not knowing what's going on. That old broad gives me the creeps."

"I'm sorry Trevor. We should have been keeping you up to date. At this point, Judge Lambert is being held in a lock down unit receiving psychiatric assessments. It looks like she won't be competent to stand trial however she will not be seeing the light of day outside of the facility where she is being held. I think we will be able to close this case out within the next few weeks. How are you holding up?"

"All things considered, pretty well. This feels almost surreal. Poor Carson. I mean she could have come for me first- way too close..." he muttered. "I can't thank you and Arnie enough for all you did. How is your aunt doing?"

"She's well, thanks. Aunt Alice has always been resilient. This case was a little too close to home that's for sure. Is there anything we can do for you at this point?"

"No. No I'm good now. I'm going to take a little time off myself and do a "staycation" here at home. I'm finishing off the final details of Carson's estate. I donated his furniture to Habitat for Humanity and after paying off his final expenses have decided to give the remaining money to a local halfway house for teenagers who are in rehab for drug and alcohol abuse. Kind of full circle, ya know?"

"That's great Trevor. God knows these kids can use all the help we can give them. We are seeing more and more heroin overdoses here even in our little town. Scary times."

"I agree," Trevor said sadly. "It makes our frat parties seem mild. Not to say that what we did wasn't wrong," he quickly recanted.

"If something good comes out of Carson's death, even if it's making a difference in one kid's recovery, then it will make this whole case a little more bearable. Let Arnie and I know if you need anything. Take care of yourself. You know it wouldn't be a bad idea to find someone to talk to professionally. This has been a pretty traumatic event for everyone."

"Thanks Lucy. I'll take that into consideration. You guys are doing a great job for your community. You take care of yourselves as well. Thanks for calling." Trevor ended the call and Lucy put the desk phone back on the cradle and returned to her unfinished files.

CHAPTER SIXTY-TWO

Lucy packed up her purse and headed out the door at about 6:00. She figured rush hour traffic would have thinned out by now and was relieved to find she was right. She and Harry had a date at 7:00 so she had plenty of time to grab a quick shower, walk and feed Quigley before he arrived.

She was just spraying on some cologne when her doorbell rang. She answered the door to see Harry standing there with a bouquet of flowers and a bottle of wine.

"How lovely," she said as she took the flowers and gave him a quick kiss. "What's the occasion?"

"It's our three-month anniversary," Harry smiled.

"And you still haven't run for the hills?" Lucy laughed as she pulled a vase out from under her sink and began filling it with water.

"What? And miss all this fun?" Harry smiled. "Seriously Lucy, I'm a lucky guy to have met you." He pulled her in his arms and gave her a long, deep kiss.

"Wow!" she said pulling back and looking into his eyes. "Keep that up and we won't be leaving the house tonight."

"Promises, promises but hold that thought. I have another surprise for you." He leaned over and patted Quigley on the head who immediately rolled over for Harry to rub his belly.

Harry laughed and picked Quigley up. "Maybe later buddy." He put him on the couch, Lucy grabbed her purse and stepped back for Harry to look at her.

"Am I dressed appropriately for your surprise?" she asked.

"Perfect!" he answered and opened the door for Lucy then closed it firmly behind him, checking to be sure it was locked.

Harry headed west on route 2, reached over and grabbed Lucy's hand and brought it to his lips and kissed it.

"Harry," Lucy laughed. "What's with you tonight? You are quite the romantic."

Harry squeezed her hand. "I'm just excited to show you my surprise. I feel like a kid at Christmas."

"So how long until we get to your 'surprise'?" she asked. "I can't imagine what this is all about."

"Not much longer" he said, as he took the exit ramp and turned right. About 10 minutes later he turned into a driveway that led them into the woods and up to a beautiful log cabin home.

"You bought a new house?" she asked in amazement.

Harry laughed. "Nope, but I certainly wouldn't mind owning this piece of property."

They got out of the car and the front door opened. A young couple stepped out and waited for Harry and Lucy to step on to the porch.

Harry held out his arm and shook their hands. "Hi folks, I'm Harry Smith and this is Lucy Amos. Lucy has no idea why we're here," he finished and winked at the woman.

"Hi Harry and Lucy. I'm Erika and this is my husband Vic. Come on in."

Lucy looked at Harry inquisitively. Harry took her elbow and led her into the house.

Following the couple into a large kitchen, Lucy's eyes were drawn to a small crate. Looking more closely she saw a dog with about 5 newborn puppies nestled around her.

"On my goodness!"

Erika smiled at her and motioned for her to come over to the crate.

"This is Princess and her new litter. They were born about 4 weeks ago."

"They are precious!" Lucy said leaning in for a better look. "Are they pugs?"

"Yes. Are you familiar with the breed?"

"I sure am. I have a pug myself."

She turned and looked at Harry. "You're buying a dog!"

"Yep. I just need you to help me to pick one out."

Lucy grinned. "I'd love to help you."

She turned to Erika and Vic. "Are any of them spoken for yet before I fall in love?"

Erika smiled. "No, I told Harry he would have the first pick. I just need to know if you want a male or female."

"I thought I'd get a little girl so Studley and she could double date with us," he joked.

Erika picked out 3 female puppies and laid them side by side on a blanket for Harry and Lucy to see.

One of the puppies managed to squirm away from her sisters and looked up at Harry.

Erika laughed. "It looks like the decision has been made for you!"

Harry scooped up the little dog and held her out in front of him eye to eye. He brought her up to his face and she began licking his nose.

Lucy put her hands to her cheeks and said "That is the cutest thing I have seen in a long time. Harry if you don't take her, I will."

"She'll be available in about 4 more weeks if you want her." Vic said, putting the other two puppies back by their mother.

Harry frowned. "Four weeks? Oh, man..."

Everyone laughed at his disappointment.

Lucy took the puppy, gave it a quick kiss on top of its head and handed her back to Erika.

She patted Harry on the back and said soothingly as if speaking to a child, "It's ok sweetie. It will give you time to pick out her bed, some toys, and all the other things she'll need when she comes home with you."

Harry played along and looked down at the floor. "OK," he said as if trying not to cry.

Looking back up at Erika and Vic he said in his normal voice "How much did you say you wanted for her?"

"We normally ask $1,000 per puppy but since she appears to be the runt of the litter, we'll take $800."

Harry opened his wallet and peeled out 8 one-hundred-dollar bills.

Vic took the money while Erika made out a receipt. "We'll make sure she gets her first round of shots by the time you pick her up."

"Thanks! I'll be back in about 4 weeks to pick you up, Fiona," he said bending over to pet his new puppy.

"Fiona? You already have her name picked out! That's hysterical," laughed Lucy as she and Harry shook Erika and Vic's hands again to seal the deal.

Harry handed Lucy his I Phone and picked Fiona up again. "Take a picture of us," he said.

Lucy took a couple of different shots, made sure they came out ok and handed Harry his phone back.

"We ok to go now, or do you want to give her another kiss?" she joked.

"Very funny. I want you to know that this is my very first dog."

"What???" everyone said together.

"We were on the move a lot with my dad's job with the band, so I never had a chance to get a dog or a cat. I did have a pet hamster...." He finished lamely.

"Wow," said Lucy. "Looks like we have some work to do. Next stop – Pet Smart."

Erika promised to give Harry a call as soon as Fiona had been weaned from her mother and Harry and Lucy headed to the pet store.

CHAPTER SIXTY-THREE

Because Judge Audrey Lambert did not attempt to deny the fact that she murdered Carson James and was guilty of the kidnapping and attempted murder of Alice Campana, charges were filed, and she pled guilty at her arraignment. A sentencing hearing was held where her lawyer pled guilty by reason of insanity. The Judge imposed a sentence of 35 years to life with no chance for parole.

Audrey Lambert would essentially serve out the remainder of her life at the Correctional Facility in Lucasville. She would be confined to the psychiatric unit of the prison until she was considered stabilized and would serve the remainder of her sentence in prison.

There was a renewed flurry of media interest at the Manor with reporters seeking out interviews with Alice for her comments on the sentencing. At Alice's request, she declined to speak with anyone and after numerous failed attempts to speak with her they moved on to the next story of the day. Robin and William Dunahie worked overtime in repeating their rehearsed talking points. "Ms. Campana and we at Elmhurst Manor are satisfied with the court's decision and are ready to put this behind us and get on with our daily routines. We thank you all for your concern and support during this unprecedented event."

Arnie made a phone call to Trevor Rathbun to share the final outcome of the hearing with Trevor breathing a sigh of relief at the news.

"Thanks for calling Arnie," he said. "If you or Lucy are ever out my way, make sure you let me know. I'd like to buy you dinner."

"Thanks Trevor. We'll take you up on that!"

"By the way," Trevor added "I have been inundated with the press up here. My gosh, they've asked me everything about myself except for my shoe size! I'm hoping now that the sentencing has been rendered, I'll get a reprieve from all this attention."

"I hear you," said Arnie. "I hope thing go back to normal for you soon. Good to talk to you again Trevor."

Arnie hung up and sat at his desk thinking about how one seemingly innocent rite of passage turned into such a horrendous outcome then and again 30 years later. "The sins of our youth," he muttered shaking his head.

"A penny for your thoughts," Lucy said as she walked into the office, dumping her purse on her desk and handing Arnie a Dunkin Donuts bag and cup of coffee.

"I don't care what they say about you Amos. You're alright!" Arnie said peering into the bag and pulling out a glazed donut.

"You're welcome." Lucy said as she pulled another bag from her purse. She unwrapped a bagel, took a bite and sighed as she looked at the pile of papers on her desk.

"Today I am not leaving until every piece of paper is off this desk!"

Arnie raised his eyebrows, looking at the chaos in front of him. '

"Good luck with that."

Lucy gave him the middle finger, sat down, and began shuffling papers.

Arnie's phone rang, he listened for a few moments, hung up and said, "Lieutenant Sharpe wants us in his office right away."

"Thank God," Lucy said, jumped up from her desk and headed out the door. Arnie laughed and followed her.

Hector Sharpe sat at his desk reading a document in front of him. He looked up and motioned for them to take a seat. He finished what he was reading and pushed a file towards them. "I need you two to take a ride out to the high school. The chemistry lab had a break in last night and some vandalism. In addition, some of the teachers have been finding some threatening notes."

"What kinds of threats?" asked Lucy.

"Copies are in the folder. I need you two to get on this one right away."

"Will do," said Arnie. "We'll take a look at the folder on our drive there."

"Keep me posted," said the Lieutenant and went back to what he was working on. He pulled a tootsie roll pop out of a bag in his desk drawer, looked at the wrapper and threw it in the garbage can. "I hate the orange ones," he muttered.

CHAPTER SIXTY-FOUR

The fourth of July was celebrated by the four cohorts, Lucy and Harry at Edgewater Park. After a picnic dinner hosted by the Manor for its residents and their guests, they made their way to the park to enjoy an evening of fireworks over Lake Erie. Getting there early (a little too early for Lucy and Harry's taste), they were able to find a spot on the beach to set up their lawn chairs and enjoy the show. Out in the distance they could see other firework displays from neighboring communities.

The ladies chatted amiably and continued to plan on the upcoming trip to Kellys Island. After assuring Faye that she would have access to a life preserver and that the ferry was strong enough to transport not only passengers but also their cars, she grudgingly agreed to come along.

Lucy brought Quigley who surprisingly seemed to enjoy the noise and spent his time sniffing around the beach with his little tail wagging non-stop. Harry, however, spent his time attempting to calm his new little addition who shook and shivered with every bang and flash of light.

"This wasn't such a great idea," he said as he held the little puppy against his chest. Fiona had taken up residence with Harry two weeks earlier and the two seemed to be settling into a routine.

Lucy helped him make the appropriate purchases: puppy pads, a small bed (although that was a wasted purchase as Harry had her sleep in the crook of his arm), and other essentials.

Harry ordered dog dishes with her name on it. It appeared the little dog would want for nothing.

Quigley and Fiona, after spending the first day cautiously sniffing at each other, appeared to be on their way to becoming best of friends. After Lucy and Quigley spent the weekend at Harry's , upon arriving back at her own apartment, Quigley would spend the first hour sniffing around as if searching for his new companion.

The case at the local high school turned out to be a disgruntled student who was attempting to settle a score with some teachers who he felt were treating him unfairly.

All in all, things were returning to normalcy in Elmwood, Ohio.

Out in Michigan, Trevor Rathbun was also settling back into a routine of work and relaxation. The rehab center gladly accepted the proceeds from Carson's estate, and in some way the slate was wiped clean from his youthful indiscretions.

He spent the 4th waterskiing and partying with friends, many of them noticing that he had become a little humbler. Although Trevor had never been considered as an arrogant person, the last couple of months certainly had changed his outlook on life. Taking Lucy's suggestion, he had begun working with a counselor and realized that the tragedy at the Pi Kappa Alpha house years ago had had some deep-seated effects; yet another reason to thank the two Detectives. He smiled thinking about them. They were so different from one another, yet the chemistry worked. He felt lucky to have had the good fortune to have them work on the case.

The rest of the weekend went by quickly. Although he had a lawn service take care of the mowing and trimming, Trevor was meticulous about his landscaping and spent time picking out a few weeds and making sure that the light bulbs on the spotlights around his home were all working.

One of his neighbors who was walking his dog waved when he saw Trevor and walked up his driveway. Trevor stopped his weeding, rubbed his hands on his jeans and reached out to shake the guy's hand. He couldn't remember his name but the man, took Trevor's hand in a tight grasp and said, "Frank Phillips. I live a couple of houses down," he said pointing to a white ranch.

"Of course," said Trevor. "How's it going?"

"Great. I'm just giving you a heads up that I've noticed a gray van going up and down on our street lately and wanted to let everyone know that it just seems a little suspicious. I'm probably being a little paranoid, but these days you just can't be too careful."

Trevor nodded. "Hey I appreciate that. I'll keep a look out for it. Nice to meet you."

The man shook his hand again and headed back towards the sidewalk, pulling his dog behind him who had taken the opportunity to lift his leg on Trevor's lamp post.

Trevor figured the van was just another reporter trying to catch him out to snag another interview. He went back to his weeding and headed into the house to grab a cold one.

After taking a shower, Trevor grabbed another beer and settled into his lazy boy prepared to watch the Tigers play the Indians. It was the second inning, and the Tribe was ahead by one. He began to doze in his chair and was startled awake when his doorbell rang.

"Crap," he said and got up to answer the door.

A young man with a baseball cap stood at the door holding a pizza box.

"Good evening, sir," he said holding out the box. "Here's the pizza you ordered. That will be $7.50."

Trevor looked at him and then the box being thrust in his direction. "Sorry, but you've got the wrong house. I didn't order a pizza," and began to shut the door.

The kid looked at the slip. "This is 27215 Bellevue Drive, correct?"

"Yes, it is, but I didn't order a pizza."

"Hey mister, can you give me a break? There must have been some sort of mix up, but if I come back with the pizza they'll take it out of my pay. I'll give it to you for three bucks."

Trevor smelled whiffs of the pizza coming from the box. He was a little hungry and the pizza would taste great with the beer.

"Sure, no problem," he said reaching into his pocket. He pulled out a ten-dollar bill, handed it to the kid and said, "Keep the change."

"Thanks a lot!" the young man said, shoving the bill in his pocket and headed back towards his car. He turned and waved at Trevor, who waved back and then shut the front door behind him.

He opened the box to see a large cheese, pepperoni and mushroom pizza. He went into the kitchen to grab some napkins and a paper plate and settle in to watch the rest of the game.

Adam Lambert tossed the baseball cap in the back seat of the car and headed towards the shopping center parking lot where he had parked the van. He'd ditch the stolen car and the pizza sign that he had taken off a car earlier that week at the pizza store parking lot, and head back to New York. The weeks of surveilling the street paid off in spades when he saw Trevor's garage door open that afternoon. He purchased the pizza adding the mushrooms and bingo, bango, boom – success. He loved it when a plan came together!

"Enjoy your pizza, sucker." he laughed. His Aunt Audrey would be so proud.

ACKNOWLEDGEMENT

MY THANKS to the many people who helped make this book possible.

All the people with whom I have interacted in the last 35 years in my role as a Medicare sales agent. Sharing your personal stories allowed me to take creative license by incorporating tidbits to create Alice and the gang. I continue to be inspired by all of you. Keep them coming!

A special thanks to my niece, Hannah (Left) Wright who created my bookcover!

ABOUT THE AUTHOR

Sue Brletic

Thirty five years in Medicare sales has allowed Sue the opportunity to interact with a diverse clientele. Listening to their stories gave her the inspiration to use some of their memories to create a story specific to this population. As a result, Alice, Faye, Gertie and Thelma were born. Although this is her first book, look for more upcoming adventures from this fearless foursome in "Beach Bedlam," still in progress.

Sue shares her home in Ohio with her Shitzu, Lexi. She has 3 grown children and 4 grandchildren. When she's not meeting with her Medicare members, or writing, you can find her repurposing old furniture, playing the piano or finding haunted locations to explore.

***Spoiler alert - look for paranormal events in Alice & company's next adventure!